W9-CFP-707

Grade

Triple 6 Smart

Desmond Gilling • William Young

ISBN : 1–894810–80–5

Copyright © 2004 **Popular Book Company (Canada) Limited**

Printed in China

Contents
Grade 6

Math

English

Science

Answers

Math

1 Whole Numbers

Find the answers. Write the answers in words and in expanded form.

① a. 396
   178
 + 597

b. Words: One thousand one hundred seventy one.

c. Expanded form:
   1171 = 000 + 100 + 70 + 1

② a. 82 651
   − 7 752

b. Words: Four million four thousand eight hundred ninety nine.

c. Expanded form:
   7 899 = 7 000 + 4000 + 800 + 90 + 9

③ a. 328
   x 76

b. Words: Two hundred twenty one thousand twenty eight

c. Expanded form:
   200 + 4000 + 900 + 20 + 8

④ a. 14)2870

b. Words: Two hundred five

c. Expanded form:
   200 + 5

Estimate the answers.

$514 \times 48 =$ _____

round to the nearest 100   round to the nearest 10

$500 \times 50 = 25\,000$

The product of 514 and 48 is close to 25 000.

$3895 \div 32 =$ _____

round to the nearest 100   round to the nearest 10

$3900 \div 30 = 130$

The quotient of 3895 ÷ 32 is close to 130.

Estimate the products first by rounding the numbers to the nearest 10 or 100. Then find the exact answers.

⑤ $596 \times 32 =$ _____ $\underline{\ 600\ } \times \underline{\ 30\ } =$ _____

⑥ $189 \times 64 =$ _____   _____ × _____ = _____

⑦ $225 \times 86 =$ _____   _____ × _____ = _____

⑧ $479 \times 73 =$ _____   _____ × _____ = _____

Estimate the quotients first by rounding the numbers to the nearest 10 or 100. Then find the exact answers.

⑨ $6482 \div 48 =$ _____ $\underline{\ 6500\ } \div \underline{\ 50\ } =$ _____

⑩ $5206 \div 19 =$ _____   _____ ÷ _____ = _____

⑪ $4788 \div 62 =$ _____   _____ ÷ _____ = _____

⑫ $3045 \div 33 =$ _____   _____ ÷ _____ = _____

Find the answers.

⑬ $12\,683 + 1594 =$ _____

⑭ $62\,008 - 7469 =$ _____

⑮ $18\,104 - 6233 =$ _____   ⑯ $6549 + 1889 =$ _____

⑰ $324 \times 55 =$ _____   ⑱ $7064 \div 34 =$ _____

⑲ $429 \times 18 =$ _____   ⑳ $5206 \div 22 =$ _____

㉑ $587 \times 46 =$ _____   ㉒ $4848 \div 45 =$ _____

Solve the problems. Show your work.

㉓ Mrs. Young has 3268 chocolate eggs. If she puts them equally into 64 baskets, how many chocolate eggs are there in each basket? How many are left?

㉔ A bag contains 52 chocolate eggs. Amy buys 125 bags. How many chocolate eggs does Amy buy in all?

㉕ Uncle Tom's store orders 18 682 small bags and 4753 big bags of chocolate eggs. How many bags of chocolate eggs does the store order in all?

㉖ Each small bag of chocolate eggs costs $12. How much will Uncle Tom get from selling 268 bags of chocolate eggs?

㉗ Joe has 7826 g of chocolate eggs. If, after buying a bag of chocolate eggs, Joe has 10 382 g, how heavy is that bag of chocolate eggs?

Calculate. Use the correct order of operations.

㉘　32 – 4 x 3

= _____ – _____

= _____

㉙　25 + 5 x 2

= _____ + _____

= _____

㉚　50 – 26 ÷ 2

= _____ – _____

= _____

㉛　16 x 2 + 15

= _____

= _____

㉜　44 ÷ 4 – 3

= _____

= _____

㉝　36 + 28 ÷ 4

= _____

= _____

㉞　56 – 42 ÷ 6

= _____

= _____

㉟　30 + 5 x 4

= _____

= _____

㊱　24 ÷ 3 + 21

= _____

= _____

Solve the problems. Show your work.

㊲　Each box of crayons costs $9. Joe pays $50 for 3 boxes of crayons. What is his change?

㊳　Jimmy shares 84 marbles with 2 friends. Then he gives 9 marbles to his brother. How many marbles does he have left?

㊴　Elaine has 1 $20 bill and 17 toonies. How much does she have?

2 Decimals

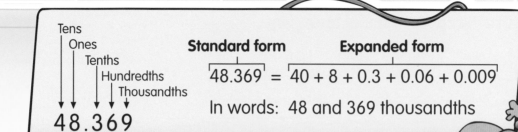

Tens
Ones
Tenths
Hundredths
Thousandths

48.369

Standard form   **Expanded form**

48.369 = 40 + 8 + 0.3 + 0.06 + 0.009

In words: 48 and 369 thousandths

Write each decimal number in expanded form and in words.

① 16.258 Expanded form: _____

Words: _____

② 23.174 Expanded form: _____

Words: _____

③ 40.019 Expanded form: _____

Words: _____

Put each group in order from least to greatest.

④ 9.854   4.958   9.548   8.549   _____

⑤ 10.204   10.402   4.102   4.201   _____

⑥ 3.175   3.715   3.751   3.157   _____

Place the following decimal numbers on the number line below.

⑦ **0.024**   **0.003**   **0.036**   **0.019**   **0.008**   **0.031**

0.024
↓

0   0.01   0.02   0.03   0.04

When adding or subtracting decimal numbers, remember to align the decimal points.

```
  2.974
+ 3.25  ✗
```

```
  2.974        0 is a place holder.
+ 3.250 ✓
```

Add or subtract.

⑧ 3.168 + 7.425 = _____

⑨ 4.639 – 1.425 = _____

⑩ 4.7 + 1.822 = _____

⑪ 5.04 – 3.288 = _____

⑫ 6.14 – 4.409 = _____

⑬ 2.083 + 3.89 = _____

⑭ 5.084 – 1.66 = _____

⑮ 4.25 + 1.745 = _____

⑯ 6.835 + 1.74 = _____

⑰ 8.7 – 6.684 = _____

⑱ 5.73 – 1.065 = _____

⑲ 9.236 – 5.67 = _____

Fill in the missing numbers.

⑳

8. ☐ 2 ☐ + ☐ . 3 ☐ 8 = 12.707

Find the products mentally.

㉑ 4.6 x 100 = _____

㉒ 3.293 x 10 = _____

㉓ 0.18 x 10 = _____

㉔ 1.47 x 100 = _____

㉕ 3.153 x 10 = _____

㉖ 2.06 x 100 = _____

> **x 10** – Move the decimal point 1 place to the right.
> e.g. 2.53 x 10 = <u>25.3</u>
>
> **x 100** – Move the decimal point 2 places to the right.
> e.g. 14.75 x 100 = <u>1475</u>

Find the products.

㉗ 9.32 x 9 = _____

㉘ 1.71 x 8 = _____

㉙ 8.83 x 6 = _____

㉚ 2.542 x 3 = _____

㉛ 1.547 x 5 = _____

㉜ 6.236 x 4 = _____

> When multiplying a decimal number and a whole number, remember to place the decimal point in the product.
>
> e.g.
> ```
>      3.46  ← 2 decimal places
>    ×    4
>    13.84  ← 2 decimal places
> ```

Find the quotients mentally.

1 zero

↓

$13.47 ÷ 10 = 1.347$

Move the decimal point 1 place to the left.

2 zeroes

↓

$208.5 ÷ 100 = 2.085$

Move the decimal point 2 places to the left.

㉝ $10.84 ÷ 10 \quad = \underline{\hspace{2cm}}$

㉞ $56.2 ÷ 100 = \underline{\hspace{2cm}}$

㉟ $230.9 ÷ 100 \quad = \underline{\hspace{2cm}}$

㊱ $462.5 ÷ 10 = \underline{\hspace{2cm}}$

㊲ $601.5 ÷ 10 \quad = \underline{\hspace{2cm}}$

㊳ $30.14 ÷ 10 = \underline{\hspace{2cm}}$

㊴ $433 ÷ 100 \quad = \underline{\hspace{2cm}}$

㊵ $20 ÷ 100 \quad = \underline{\hspace{2cm}}$

㊶ $16.5 ÷ 10 \quad = \underline{\hspace{2cm}}$

㊷ $25.6 ÷ 100 = \underline{\hspace{2cm}}$

㊸ $0.25 ÷ 10 \quad = \underline{\hspace{2cm}}$

㊹ $5.4 ÷ 10 \quad = \underline{\hspace{2cm}}$

㊺ $37 ÷ 100 \quad = \underline{\hspace{2cm}}$

㊻ $40 ÷ 100 \quad = \underline{\hspace{2cm}}$

Find the quotients.

㊼ $6 \overline{) 109.8}$

㊽ $8 \overline{) 181.92}$

㊾ $5 \overline{) 84.15}$

㊿ $51.31 ÷ 7 \quad = \underline{\hspace{2cm}}$

51 $70.16 ÷ 2 \quad = \underline{\hspace{2cm}}$

52 $14.61 ÷ 3 \quad = \underline{\hspace{2cm}}$

53 $115.52 ÷ 4 \quad = \underline{\hspace{2cm}}$

54 $20.24 ÷ 8 \quad = \underline{\hspace{2cm}}$

55 $374.13 ÷ 9 \quad = \underline{\hspace{2cm}}$

56 $450.36 ÷ 6 \quad = \underline{\hspace{2cm}}$

Put a decimal point in the quotient above the one in the dividend.

Don't forget to put a zero in the quotient as a place holder.

$$7 \overline{) \begin{array}{c} 25.06 \\ 175.42 \end{array}}$$
$$\begin{array}{r} 14 \\ \hline 35 \\ 35 \\ \hline 42 \\ 42 \end{array}$$

57 $42.72 ÷ 4 \quad = \underline{\hspace{2cm}}$

58 $537.75 ÷ 5 \quad = \underline{\hspace{2cm}}$

59 $140.28 ÷ 7 \quad = \underline{\hspace{2cm}}$

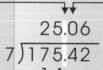

Solve the problems. Show your work.

This Week's Specials

60 How much do 4 boxes of cookies weigh?

61 How much is 1 chicken burger?

62 There are 7 slices of corned beef in one pack. How heavy is one slice of corned beef?

63 Andy buys 1 tub of ice cream and 1 pack of corned beef. How much does he need to pay?

64 Ted buys 3 boxes of chicken burgers for his family. How much does he need to pay?

65 Uncle Bill pays $20 for 1 tub of ice cream. What is his change?

My sister and I buy a tub of ice cream for Darren the Cat. I pay $1.15 more than my sister. How much does my sister have to pay?

66 She has to pay $ _____ .

3 Fractions, Percent, and Ratio

Change the improper fractions to mixed numbers and the mixed numbers to improper fractions.

improper fraction → mixed number

$$\frac{7}{4} = 1\frac{3}{4} \qquad 4\overline{)7} \;\; \begin{array}{c} 1 \\ \underline{4} \\ 3 \end{array}$$

mixed number → improper fraction

$$1\frac{3}{4} = \frac{1 \times 4 + 3}{4} = \frac{7}{4}$$

① $\dfrac{5}{3}$ = _____ ② $\dfrac{16}{5}$ = _____

③ $4\dfrac{1}{2}$ = _____ ④ $3\dfrac{2}{7}$ = _____

⑤ $1\dfrac{4}{5}$ = _____ ⑥ $\dfrac{8}{7}$ = _____ ⑦ $2\dfrac{3}{4}$ = _____

⑧ $3\dfrac{1}{10}$ = _____ ⑨ $\dfrac{15}{8}$ = _____ ⑩ $\dfrac{11}{6}$ = _____

Compare the fractions. Put > or < in the circles.

⑪ $\dfrac{9}{8}$ ◯ $\dfrac{5}{8}$ ⑫ $\dfrac{3}{11}$ ◯ $\dfrac{3}{10}$ ⑬ $\dfrac{4}{5}$ ◯ $\dfrac{4}{7}$

⑭ $\dfrac{15}{16}$ ◯ $\dfrac{13}{16}$ ⑮ $\dfrac{17}{25}$ ◯ $\dfrac{11}{25}$ ⑯ $\dfrac{12}{19}$ ◯ $\dfrac{12}{13}$

Put the fractions in order from least to greatest.

⑰ $\dfrac{5}{2}$ $1\dfrac{1}{2}$ $\dfrac{3}{4}$ _____

⑱ $\dfrac{19}{7}$ $2\dfrac{1}{7}$ $1\dfrac{6}{7}$ _____

⑲ $3\dfrac{1}{10}$ $\dfrac{19}{10}$ $1\dfrac{3}{5}$ _____

⑳ $1\dfrac{5}{6}$ $\dfrac{7}{3}$ $\dfrac{13}{6}$ _____

Comparing fractions:

1st Write fractions as mixed numbers.

2nd Compare the whole numbers. If they are the same, go to 3rd.

3rd Compare the fractions. Write fractions with like denominator; then compare the numerators.

Use fractions to complete the addition or subtraction sentences. Write the answers in simplest form.

㉑ 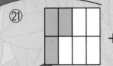 + =

____ + ____ = ____

㉒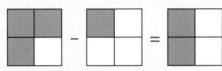

____ - ____ = ____

㉓  + 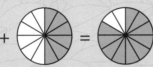 =

____ + ____ = ____

㉔

____ - ____ = ____

> *When adding or subtracting fractions with the same denominator, add or subtract the numerators. Remember to reduce the answers to simplest form.*

Find the sums or differences. Then write the answers in simplest form.

㉕ $\dfrac{14}{15} - \dfrac{9}{15} =$ ____ = ____

㉖ $\dfrac{3}{10} + \dfrac{3}{10} =$ ____ = ____

㉗ $\dfrac{7}{20} + \dfrac{9}{20} =$ ____ = ____

㉘ $\dfrac{8}{9} - \dfrac{5}{9} =$ ____ = ____

㉙ $\dfrac{3}{8} + \dfrac{1}{8} =$ ____ = ____

㉚ $\dfrac{11}{12} - \dfrac{7}{12} =$ ____ = ____

㉛ $\dfrac{9}{14} + \dfrac{3}{14} =$ ____ = ____

㉜ $\dfrac{7}{8} - \dfrac{1}{8} =$ ____ = ____

㉝ $\dfrac{5}{16} + \dfrac{7}{16} =$ ____ = ____

㉞ $\dfrac{13}{18} - \dfrac{1}{18} =$ ____ = ____

㉟ $\dfrac{19}{24} - \dfrac{1}{24} =$ ____ = ____

㊱ $\dfrac{7}{13} + \dfrac{6}{13} =$ ____ = ____

㊲ $\dfrac{9}{10} - \dfrac{3}{10} =$ ____ = ____

㊳ $\dfrac{17}{20} - \dfrac{3}{20} =$ ____ = ____

Rewrite each of the following using %.

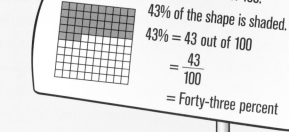

Percent (%) means a part of 100.
43% of the shape is shaded.
43% = 43 out of 100
$= \frac{43}{100}$
= Forty-three percent

㊴ Thirty-one percent = _____

㊵ Eighty-six percent = _____

㊶ 36 out of 100 = _____   ㊷ 25 out of 100 = _____

㊸ $\frac{49}{100} =$ _____   ㊹ $\frac{6}{100} =$ _____   ㊺ $\frac{13}{100} =$ _____

Write the percent that represents the shaded part of each 100-square grid.

㊻

㊼

Rewrite the fractions with 100 as the denominator. Then write them as %.

㊽ $\frac{3}{5} =$ _____ = _____ %   ㊾ $\frac{9}{20} =$ _____ = _____ %

㊿ $\frac{1}{4} =$ _____ = _____ %   51 $\frac{7}{10} =$ _____ = _____ %

Rewrite the percent as fractions in simplest form.

52 68% = _____   53 70% = _____   54 50% = _____

55 45% = _____   56 24% = _____   57 30% = _____

Rewrite the percent as decimals.

58 26% = _____   59 40% = _____   60 18% = _____

61 9% = _____   62 63% = _____   63 55% = _____

*Write the percent as fractions with 100 in the
denominator first. Then write the fractions as decimals.*

Find the rates.

64   8 piles for $59.20

$ _____ /pile

65   13.2 kg for 4 bags

_____ kg/bag

66   26.4 L for 3 days

_____ L/day

67   3 bunches for $11.01

$ _____ /bunch

Look at the pictures. Write the ratios.

68

   a.   apples to oranges   = _____

   b.   apples to all   = _____

   c.   oranges to all   = _____

> **Ratio** is a comparison between 2 or more quantities of the same unit. A ratio can be written in fraction form.
>
> e.g. $2:3 = \dfrac{2}{3}$
>
> **Equivalent ratios:**
>
>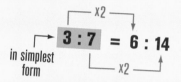
>
> $\overset{\text{in simplest form}}{3:7} = 6:14$

69

   a.   hearts to stars   = _____

   b.   hearts to all   = _____

   c.   stars to all   = _____

Write the equivalent ratios.

70   2:7   = _____

71   4:5   = _____

72   8:9 = _____

73   4:15 = _____

74   3:10 = _____

75   6:7 = _____

Write the ratios in simplest form.

76   6:18 = _____

77   2:20 = _____

78   8:12 = _____

79   10:15 = _____

80   9:21 = _____

81   12:16 = _____

82   9:12 = _____

83   6:27 = _____

84   15:25 = _____

4 Integers and Number Theory

Write the letters in the circles.

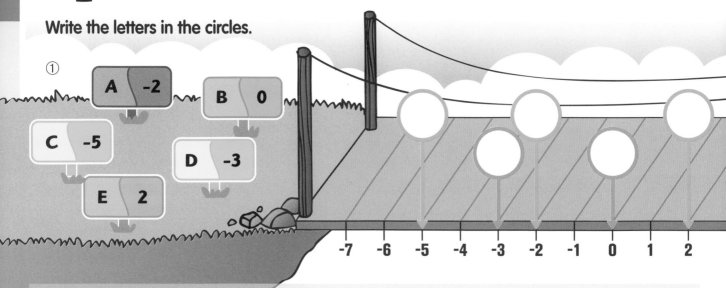

① A -2   B 0   C -5   D -3   E 2

-7 -6 -5 -4 -3 -2 -1 0 1 2

Circle the greater number in each pair.

② -4   9   ③ 1   -1   ④ -2   -3   ⑤ 4   0

⑥ 5   -5   ⑦ -6   -2   ⑧ -3   -1   ⑨ -7   0

Read the clues. Complete the table and answer the questions.

The temperature on Sunday was -2°C. The temperature on Monday was 2°C higher than that on Sunday. The temperature on Tuesday was 1°C lower than that on Sunday. The temperatures on Wednesday and Thursday were -5°C and 2°C respectively. The temperature on Friday and Saturday was the same. It was 1°C below 0°C.

⑩

	SUN	MON	TUE	WED	THU	FRI	SAT
Temperature							

⑪ Which day was the warmest? _____

⑫ Which day was the coldest? _____

⑬ In how many days were the temperatures below 0°C? _____

⑭ Which day was colder, Tuesday or Saturday? _____

⑮ Which day was warmer, Sunday or Friday? _____

Use the 50-square chart to complete the following questions.

1	2	3	4	5	6	7	8	9	10
11	12	13	14	15	16	17	18	19	20
21	22	23	24	25	26	27	28	29	30
31	32	33	34	35	36	37	38	39	40
41	42	43	44	45	46	47	48	49	50

⑯ Colour the multiples of 2 red.

⑰ Circle ◯ the multiples of 3.

⑱ Cross out ✘ the multiples of 5.

⑲ Put a △ on the multiples of 8.

⑳ Numbers with ◯ are common multiples of 2 and _____ . They

are _____ .

㉑ Numbers with △ are common multiples of _____ and _____ .

They are _____ .

㉒ The least common multiples (L.C.M.) of

    a. 2 and 3 is _____ .   b. 2 and 5 is _____ .

    c. 5 and 8 is _____ .   d. 3 and 8 is _____ .

List the first 10 multiples of each number. Then circle the common multiples of each pair of numbers and find their L.C.M.

㉓  **Multiples of 3** : 3, 6, 9, 12, ⑮, _____

    Multiples of 5 : 5, 10, ⑮, 20, _____

    The L.C.M. of 3 and 5 is _____ .

㉔ **Multiples of 4** : _____

    Multiples of 6 : _____

    The L.C.M. of 4 and 6 is _____ .

19

Use multiplication or division to find the factors of a number.

e.g. 10 = 1 x 10

= 2 x 5

1, 2, 5, and 10 are factors of 10.

**Complete the multiplication or division sentences.
Then list all the factors of each number.**

㉕ 12 = 1 x _____

= 2 x _____

= 3 x _____

㉖ 20 ÷ 1 = _____

20 ÷ 2 = _____

20 ÷ 4 = _____

㉗ 16 = 1 x _____

= 2 x _____

= 4 x _____

㉘ 36 = 1 x _____

= 2 x _____

= 3 x _____

= 4 x _____

= 6 x _____

㉙ 24 ÷ 1 = _____

24 ÷ 2 = _____

24 ÷ 3 = _____

24 ÷ 4 = _____

㉚ 48 ÷ 1 = _____

48 ÷ 2 = _____

48 ÷ 3 = _____

48 ÷ 4 = _____

48 ÷ 6 = _____

㉛ a. Factors of 12: _____

b. Factors of 20: _____

c. Factors of 16: _____

d. Factors of 36: _____

e. Factors of 24: _____

f. Factors of 48: _____

Refer to ㉛ . List the common factors of each group of numbers and find the grestest common factor (G.C.F.).

㉜ **12** and **20** Common factors: _____ G.C.F.: _____

㉝ **16** and **36** Common factors: _____ G.C.F.: _____

㉞ **24** and **48** Common factors: _____ G.C.F.: _____

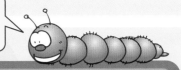

Circle the prime numbers.

㉟ 9   17   25   29   30   36   38   39   41

      56   64   68   70   73   74   86   95   97

Complete the factor trees and write each number as a product of prime factors.

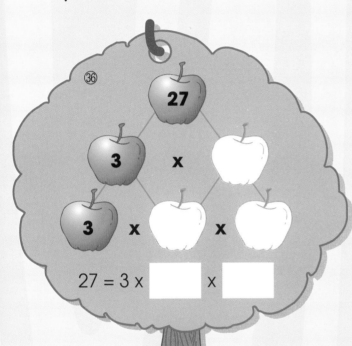

㊱ 27

3 × ☐

3 × ☐ × ☐

27 = 3 × ☐ × ☐

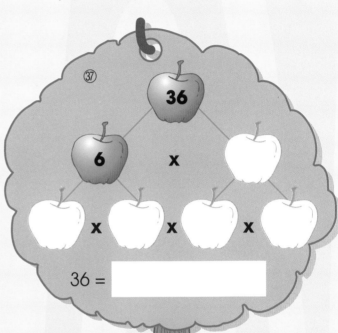

㊲ 36

6 × ☐

☐ × ☐ × ☐ × ☐

36 = ☐

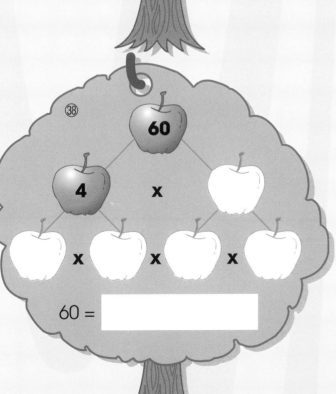

㊳ 60

4 × ☐

☐ × ☐ × ☐ × ☐

60 = ☐

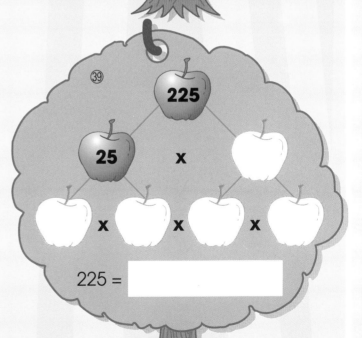

㊴ 225

25 × ☐

☐ × ☐ × ☐ × ☐

225 = ☐

21

5 Measurement

Parallelogram

Area of a parallelogram
= base x height

Triangle

Area of a triangle
= base x height ÷ 2

Find the perimeters (P) and areas (A) of the figures. Show your work.

①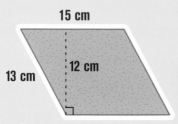

15 cm

12 cm

13 cm

P: _____ = _____ cm

A: _____ = _____ cm²

②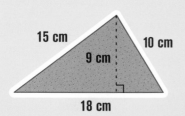

15 cm   10 cm

9 cm

18 cm

P: _____ = _____ cm

A: _____ = _____ cm²

③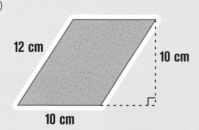

12 cm

10 cm

10 cm

P: _____ = _____ cm

A: _____ = _____ cm²

④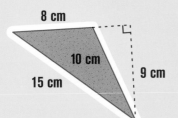

8 cm

10 cm

9 cm

15 cm

P: _____ = _____ cm

A: _____ = _____ cm²

⑤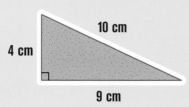

10 cm

4 cm

9 cm

P: _____ = _____ cm

A: _____ = _____ cm²

Draw 3 different parallelograms, each having an area of 12 cm².

1 cm

1 cm

⑥

Draw 3 different triangles, each having an area of 6 cm².

⑦

For question ⑪, you can draw a line on the shape to cut it into the shapes that you are familiarized with. Then find and add the areas of the shapes to work out the answer.

Solve the problems.

⑧ The height of the parallelogram is 2 times of its base. What is the area of this parallelogram?

4 cm

_____ cm²

⑨ The 3 sides of the triangle are 8 cm, 9 cm, and 12 cm. What is its area?

_____ cm²

⑩ If the base of the parallelogram is 6 cm, what is its height?

48 cm²

_____ cm

⑪ What is the area of this shape?

3 cm

9 cm

6 cm

4 cm

_____ cm²

Find the volumes of the rectangular prisms.

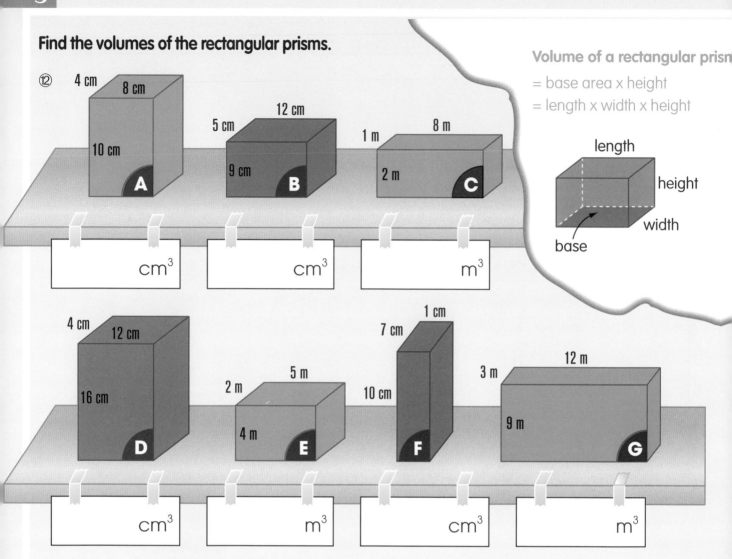

⑫

A _____ cm³

B _____ cm³

C _____ m³

D _____ cm³

E _____ m³

F _____ cm³

G _____ m³

Volume of a rectangular prism
= base area x height
= length x width x height

Find the missing information for each rectangular prism.

⑬ Base area: 27 cm²

Volume: 108 cm³

Height: _____ cm

⑭ Height: 12 m

Volume: 180 m³

Base area: _____ m²

⑮ Base area: 39 cm²

Volume: 234 cm³

Height: _____ cm

⑯ Height: 9 m

Volume: 112.5 m³

Base area: _____ m²

Find the volumes.

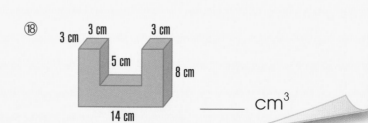

⑰ _____ cm³

⑱ _____ cm³

Circle the most appropriate unit for measuring the mass of each item.

⑲ A bag of carrots

mg   g   kg

⑳ A pill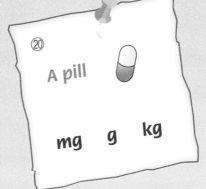

mg   g   kg

㉑ An onion

mg   g   kg

㉒ A leaf

mg   g   kg

㉓ A mug

mg   g   kg

㉔ A man

mg   g   kg

1 kilogram = 1000 grams
1 kg = 1000 g

1 gram = 1000 milligrams
1 g = 1000 mg

Fill in the missing numbers.

㉕ 2 kg = _____ g

㉖ 250 mg = _____ g

㉗ 6.8 kg = _____ g

㉘ 4000 mg = _____ g

㉙ 3 g   = _____ mg

㉚ 400 g   = _____ kg

㉛ 0.5 g = _____ mg

㉜ 6000 g = _____ kg

Answer the questions.

㉝   A bottle weighs 50 g and a tablet weighs 450 mg.
     What is the mass of a bottle with 100 tablets in g?   _____ g

㉞   A bag of candies weighs 800 g. What is the mass
     of 5 bags of candies in kg?   _____ kg

㉟   The mass of 50 cookies is 2.5 kg. What is the mass
     of 1 cookie in g?   _____ g

6 Geometry

Use the lines of symmetry (dotted lines) to complete each shape.

①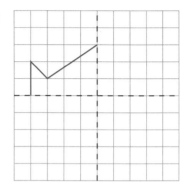

②

③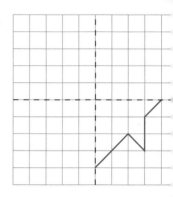

④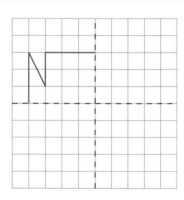

⑤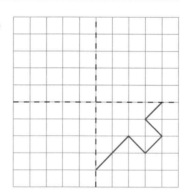

⑥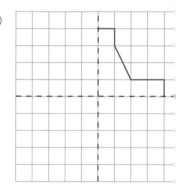

Add the minimum number of squares to each shape to make it symmetrical. Draw the squares.

⑦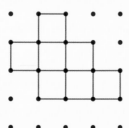

⑧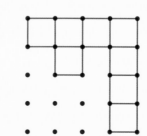

⑨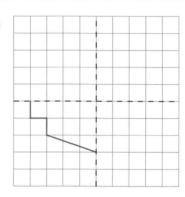

⑩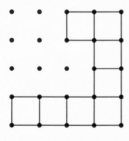

⑪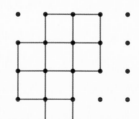

⑫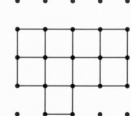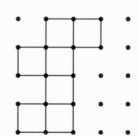

Write the order of rotational symmetry for each shape.

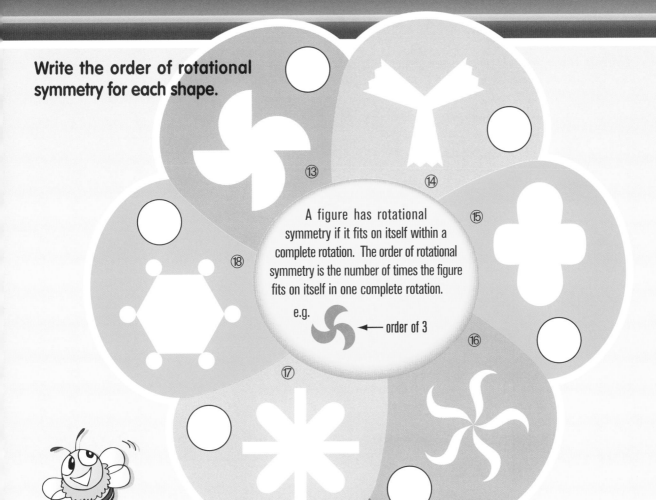

A figure has rotational symmetry if it fits on itself within a complete rotation. The order of rotational symmetry is the number of times the figure fits on itself in one complete rotation.

e.g. ← order of 3

Use a protractor and a ruler to construct the shapes.

⑲ Draw a triangle with no line of symmetry.

⑳ Draw a triangle with angles of 40°, 50°, and 90°.

㉑ Draw a square with sides of 2 cm. Then cut it into 4 identical rectangles.

㉒ Complete the figure so that it has 2 lines of symmetry.

27

Colour the congruent figures yellow and the similar ones blue.

㉓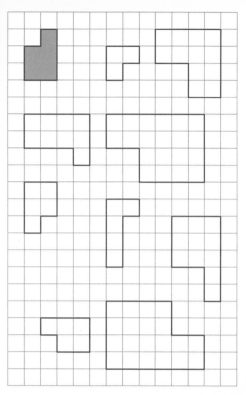

㉔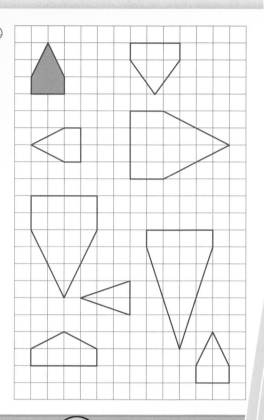

Complete the net for each solid.

㉕ Triangular pyramid

㉖ Hexagonal pyramid

㉗ Rectangular prism

㉘ Pentagonal prism

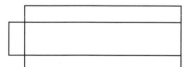

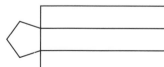

Tommy has built some models with interlocking cubes. Help him draw the models on the isometric dot paper. Then draw the top view, side view, and front view.

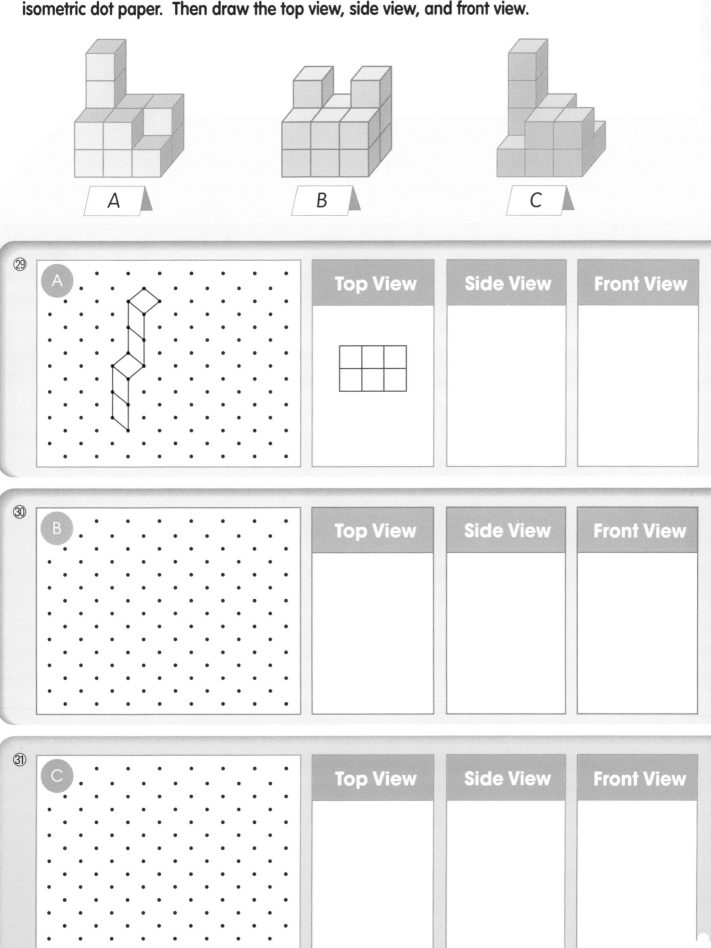

A

B

C

㉙

A

| Top View | Side View | Front View |

㉚

B

| Top View | Side View | Front View |

㉛

C

| Top View | Side View | Front View |

7 Transformations and Coordinates

The red figures are translation images. Describe the movement in each translation.

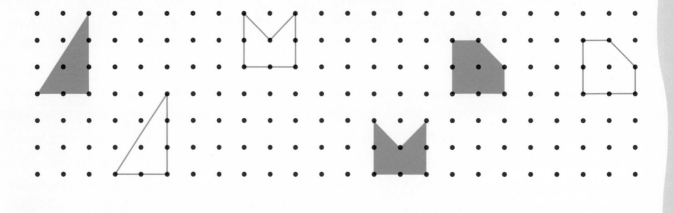

① _____   ② _____   ③ _____

The green figures are reflection images. Draw the line of reflection in each reflection.

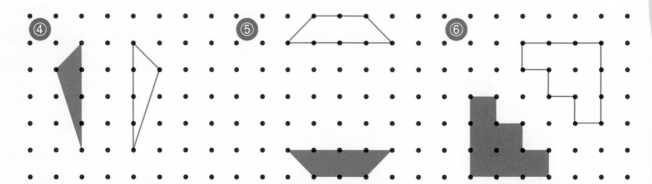

The blue figures are rotation images. Mark the centre of each rotation with a cross **✗** .

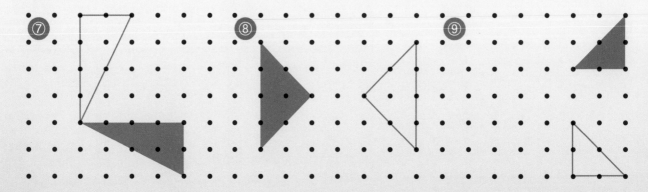

Draw the transformed images and answer the questions.

⑩ a. Translate the rectangle 2 units right and 5 units down, and colour it green.

b. Reflect the green rectangle over ℓ and colour it red.

c. What transformation can you use to move the red rectangle onto the yellow one?

_____

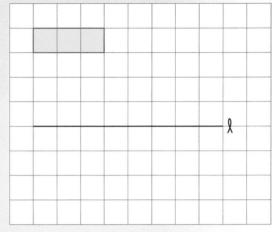

⑪ a. Reflect the triangle over ℓ and colour it red.

b. Rotate the red triangle a quarter turn counterclockwise about point P and colour it green.

c. Do the triangles have the same area?

_____

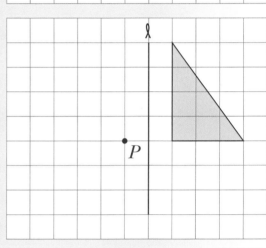

⑫ a. Rotate the triangle a quarter turn clockwise about P and colour it green.

b. Reflect the triangles over ℓ₁ and ℓ₂. Then colour them green.

c. How many lines of symmetry does the figure have?

_____

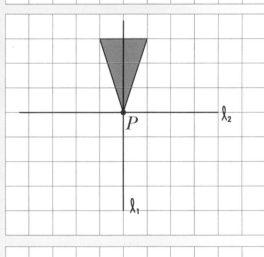

⑬ a. Rotate the triangle a half turn about P and colour it red.

b. Translate the red triangle 2 units left and the yellow triangle 2 units right.

c. Can right-angled triangles make a tiling pattern?

_____

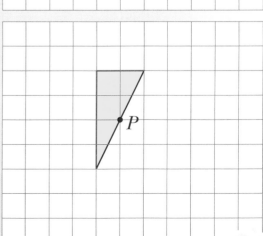

Draw the transformed images and write the coordinates. Answer the question.

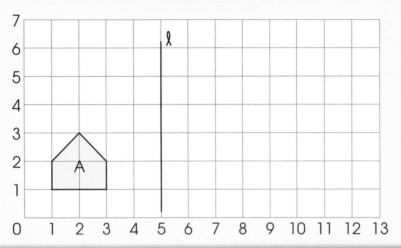

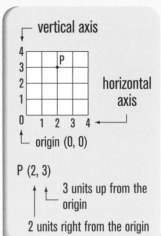

vertical axis

horizontal axis

origin (0, 0)

P (2, 3)

3 units up from the origin

2 units right from the origin

⑭ The coordinates of the vertices of A are:

_____

⑮ Reflect A over ℓ. Label the image B. The coordinates of the vertices of B are:

_____

⑯ Rotate A $\frac{1}{4}$ turn counterclockwise about (2,4). Label the image C. The coordinates of the vertices of C are:

_____

⑰ Translate B 5 units right and 1 unit up. Then rotate it $\frac{1}{4}$ turn clockwise about (13,4). Label the image D. The coordinates of the vertices of D are:

_____

⑱ If D is a reflection image of C, draw the line of reflection and label it q.

⑲ What transformations could you do to D to make A its transformed image?

_____

_____

Plot and join the points to see what shapes they are. Then answer the questions.

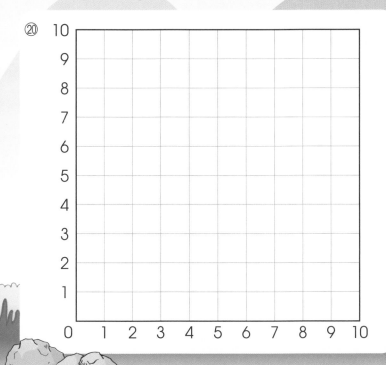

⑳

Shapes

- A (3,2), B (8, 2), C (8, 5)

- P (0, 9), Q (3, 9),
  R (5, 5), S (2, 5)

㉑ What shape is ABC? _____

㉒ What shape is PQRS? _____

㉓ What is the area of ABC? _____ square units

㉔ What is the area of PQRS? _____ square units

㉕ If S is moved 2 units left, what will its coordinates be? After the translation, what shape is PQRS?

_____

The grid shows a map of Tim's neighbourhood. Answer the questions.

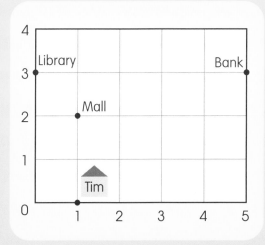

㉖ Where is the bank located?

_____

㉗ If each unit represents 100 m, what is the distance between

a. the library and the bank?

_____ m

b. the mall and Tim's house?

_____ m

33

8 Patterns and Simple Equations

Match each pattern rule with a pattern.
Write the letter. Then find the next 3 numbers.

A Double the previous number and add 1

B Triple the previous number and minus 1

C One half of the previous number and add 5

D Double the previous number and minus 3

① 7 11 19 35 _____ _____ _____   Pattern rule: ◯

② 8 17 35 71 _____ _____ _____   Pattern rule: ◯

③ 74 42 26 18 _____ _____ _____   Pattern rule: ◯

④ 3 8 23 68 _____ _____ _____   Pattern rule: ◯

Look for the patterns. Describe the rules and extend the patterns.

⑤ 2 5 11 23 _____ _____ _____

Pattern rule _____

⑥ 3 4 6 10 _____ _____ _____

Pattern rule _____

⑦ 446 222 110 54 _____ _____ _____

Pattern rule _____

34

Complete the graph to show the pattern and solve the problems.

⑧

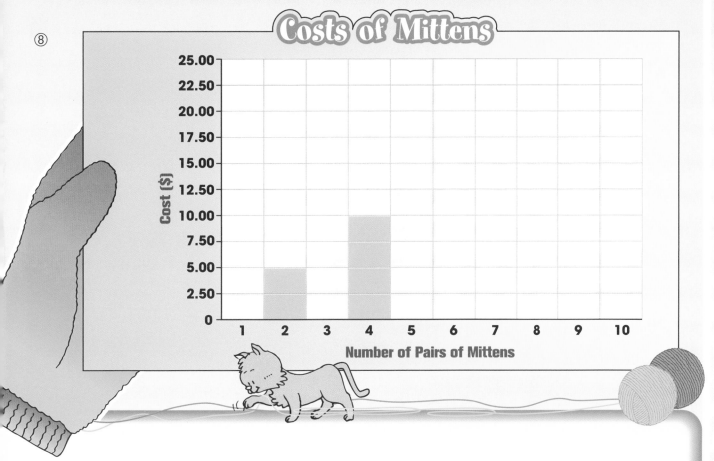

Costs of Mittens

⑨ How many pairs of mittens can be bought with $20? _____ pairs

⑩ How much do 7 pairs of mittens cost? $ _____

⑪ How much do 12 pairs of mittens cost? $ _____

⑫ Describe the pattern of the costs of mittens.

_____

⑬ If the cost of each pair of mittens is reduced to $2, does the new costs of mittens follow a pattern? If they do, what pattern do they follow?

_____

⑭ The first customer buys 2 pairs of mittens; the second buys 3 pairs; the third buys 5 pairs; the fourth buys 8 pairs.

a. Describe the pattern of the number of pairs of mittens sold.

_____

b. How many pairs of mittens will the sixth customer buy?

_____ pairs

The data in each table follow a pattern. Complete the tables and answer the questions.

⑮ The number of coupons sold:

a.

Date	Sun	Mon	Tue	Wed	Thu	Fri
Number of Coupons	50	75	100	125		

b. On which day will 200 coupons be sold? _____

c. How many coupons will be sold on the coming Monday? _____

⑯ Distance from the starting point:

a.

Time	1:00 p.m.	2:00 p.m.	3:00 p.m.	4:00 p.m.	5:00 p.m.	6:00 p.m.
Distance (km)	40	100	160	220		

b. At what time will the distance from the starting point be 400 km? _____

c. What will the distance from the starting point be at 8:00 p.m.? _____

⑰ Number of beads needed to make bracelets:

a.

Number of Bracelets	1	2	3	4	5	6
Number of Beads	64	128	192	256		

b. How many bracelets can be made with 512 beads? _____

c. How many beads are needed to make 10 bracelets? _____

Write an equation with a "y" for each problem and find the number.

⑱ 4 times a number is 20.

The number is _____ .

⑲ 3 less than a number is 9.

The number is _____ .

⑳ 5 more than a number is 15.

The number is _____ .

㉑ 50 divided by a number is 10.

The number is _____ .

Find the missing number in each equation with the help of the given equation.

㉒ 9.6 + 7.59 = 17.19

17.19 – _____ = 7.59

㉓ 125 x 26 = 3250

3250 ÷ _____ = 125

㉔ 80.17 – 16.88 = 63.29

_____ + 63.29 = 80.17

㉕ 1728 ÷ 48 = 36

_____ x 36 = 1728

Determine the value of the missing number in each equation.

㉖ 63 x _____ = 98 + 28

㉗ 35 ÷ _____ = 16 – 9

㉘ _____ + 25 = 26 + 49

㉙ _____ – 24 = 38 x 2

㉚ _____ ÷ 12 = 5 x 2

㉛ _____ x 4 = 9 + 39

Do the part without missing term first. Then "guess and test" the missing number.

9 Data Management

Lisa has made 24 paper flowers with paper. Look at the circle graph and help Lisa solve the problems.

Colour of Paper Flowers

① What fraction of the flowers are

    a.   red?   _____

    b.   yellow?   _____

    c.   blue?   _____

    d.   purple?   _____

② How many flowers does each sector in the circle graph represent?

   _____ flowers

③ Which colour of the flowers are the fewest?

   _____

④ Which colour of the flowers are the most?

   _____

Look at the circle graph again. Then complete the table and use the bar graph to show the information.

⑤

Colour	No. of Flowers
Red	
Yellow	
Blue	
Purple	

⑥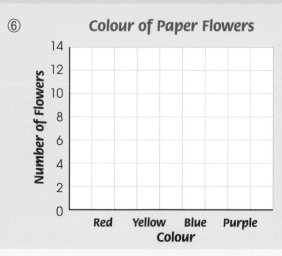

Colour of Paper Flowers

Tom and Eva did a survey to find the favourite drinks among their friends. Look at their records. Help them solve the problems.

Drink	Pop	Milk	Juice	Others
No. of People Surveyed by Tom	48	14	32	18
No. of People Surveyed by Eva	32	16	33	27

⑦ Complete the table to show Tom and Eva's findings and use a bar graph to show the information.

Drink	No. of People
Pop	
Milk	
Juice	
Others	

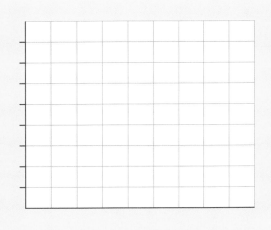

⑧ Which drink is the most popular? _____

⑨ Which drink is the least popular? _____

⑩ Does the graph tell the number of girls surveyed? _____

⑪ If 95 boys were surveyed, how many girls did Tom and Eva ask? _____

⑫ What does the word "Others" mean in the table? Suggest an example that may be included in this column.

_____

_____

Use a line graph to show the number of pizzas sold between January and October. Then solve the problems.

MONTH	Jan	Feb	Mar	Apr	May	Jun	Jul	Aug	Sep	Oct
No. of Pepperoni Pizzas Sold	400	300	200	150	200	150	200	400	500	600
No. of Hawaiian Pizzas Sold	600	600	600	600	550	550	600	550	500	500

⑬

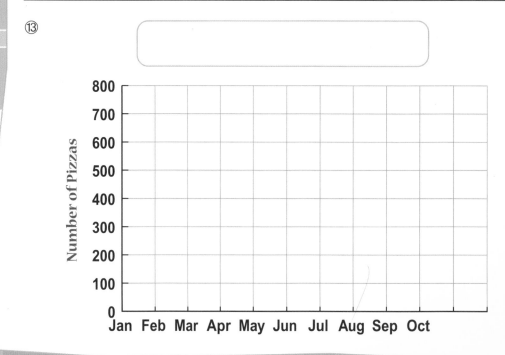

⑭ In which month was the number of Pepperoni pizzas and Hawaiian pizzas sold the same? _____

⑮ How many more Pepperoni pizzas were sold than Hawaiian pizzas in October? _____ more

⑯ Describe the sales of Pepperoni pizzas in the first 6 months.

_____

⑰ Describe the sales of Hawaiian pizzas in the first 6 months.

_____

⑱ Following the trend, estimate the number of Pepperoni pizzas sold in November. _____

Find the mean, mode, and median of each set of data.

Median:
Put the numbers in order.
2   3   ④   ⑥   6   9
Find the average of the 2 middle numbers.

Number of rats in 6 groups: 4   6   6   9   2   3

mean – average
median – middle value
mode – most common value

mean: (4+6+6+9+2+3)÷6 = 5
median: (4+6)÷2 = 5
mode: 6

---

⑲ Number of vehicles owned by 10 families:

4   1   3   2   1   2   2   1   3   1

Mean		vehicle(s)
Median		vehicle(s)
Mode		vehicle(s)

---

⑳ Number of candies in 12 bags:

12   27   14   22   15   11   18   17   22   12   12   10

Mean		candies
Median	14.5	candies
Mode	12	candies

㉑ Costs of 6 storybooks:

$18.25 $20.14 $13.09 $18.25 $12.44 $9.87

Mean	$	
Median	$	
Mode	$	

㉒ Lengths of 8 ribbons:

9.8 cm   6.4 cm   3.9 cm   7.6 cm
4.4 cm   3.9 cm   6.4 cm   6.4 cm

Mean		cm
Median		cm
Mode		cm

㉓ Find 4 numbers which are all positive integers with a mean of 6, a median of 7, and a mode of 9.

_____

10 Probability

Emily uses circle graphs to show the probabilities of picking marbles of different colours. Help her match each circle graph with the correct situation.

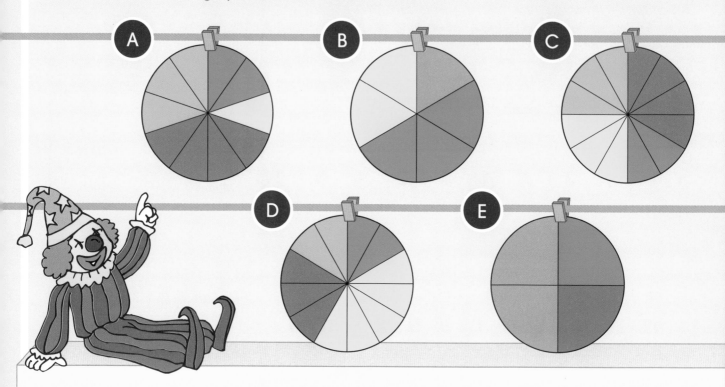

① The probability of picking a red marble is $\frac{1}{6}$, a yellow one, $\frac{5}{12}$, a green one, $\frac{1}{4}$, and an orange one, $\frac{1}{6}$.

② The probability of picking a blue marble is $\frac{1}{6}$, a red one, $\frac{1}{2}$, and a yellow one, $\frac{1}{3}$.

③ The probability of picking a blue marble is $\frac{1}{2}$. The chance of picking a red marble or a green one is the same.

④ The probability of picking a green marble is $\frac{1}{3}$ and a red one, $\frac{1}{6}$. The chance of picking a yellow marble or an orange one is the same.

⑤ The probability of picking a red marble is $\frac{1}{5}$, a yellow one, $\frac{1}{10}$, a green one, $\frac{2}{5}$, and an orange one, $\frac{3}{10}$.

Write numbers on the spinners to match the probabilities. Then fill in the blanks with fractions in simplest form to complete the sentences.

⑥

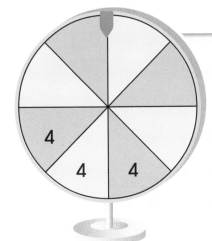

a. The probability of spinning a "2" is $\frac{1}{2}$.

b. The probability of spinning a "7" is $\frac{1}{8}$.

c. The probability of spinning an even number is _____.

⑦

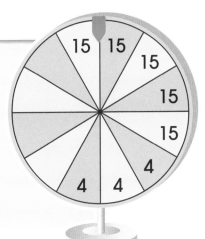

a. The probability of spinning a "10" is $\frac{1}{12}$.

b. The probability of spinning an "8" is $\frac{1}{4}$.

c. The probability of spinning a 2-digit number is _____.

⑧

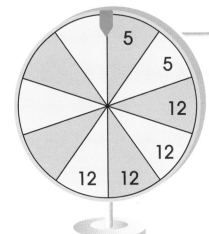

a. The probability of spinning a "20" is $\frac{1}{10}$.

b. The probability of spinning a "9" is $\frac{3}{10}$.

c. The probability of spinning a number greater than 10 is _____.

⑨

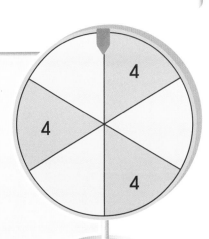

a. The probability of spinning a "5" is $\frac{1}{3}$.

b. The probability of spinning an "11" is $\frac{1}{6}$.

c. The probability of spinning a composite number is _____.

George is going to pick one ball from a bag and draw one card from a set of 4 number cards. Help him complete the tree diagram and solve the problems.

⑩   All the possible combinations:

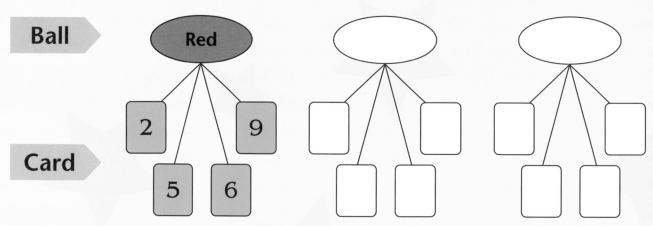

⑪   How many possible combinations are there?   _____

⑫   Is each outcome equally likely?   _____

⑬   Find the probability of each of the following.

    a. red ball and "5"   _____   b. yellow ball and "9"   _____

    c. red ball   _____   d. "2"   _____

    e. green ball and a number greater than "4"   _____

    f. yellow ball and an even number   _____

        g. green ball and a composite number   _____

        ⑭ If George plays 60 times, about how many times will he get a red ball and "9"?   _____

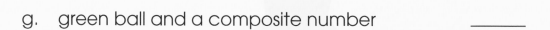

Look at the menu. Choose one item from each category and use a tree diagram to show all the possible combinations. Answer the questions.

MENU

Main Course

Hamburger **or** Sandwich

Side Dish

Salad **or** Fries

or

Baked potato

Dessert

Cake   Ice cream

⑮ All the possible combinations:

⑯ How many possible combinations are there? _____

⑰ How many combinations include cake? _____

⑱ How many combinations include fries? _____

⑲ What is the probability of a customer choosing a meal with

   a. hamburger, fries, and cake? _____

   b. sandwich, salad, and ice cream? _____

   c. pizza, baked potato, and cake? _____

Math - REVIEW

Find the quotients.

① $6\overline{)158.4}$

② $8\overline{)113.76}$

③ $2\overline{)19.56}$

Put the fractions in order from least to greatest.

⑦ $2\frac{3}{5}$ $\frac{19}{5}$ $3\frac{1}{5}$ _____

⑧ $1\frac{5}{8}$ $\frac{16}{8}$ $\frac{9}{8}$ _____

⑨ $\frac{11}{4}$ $1\frac{3}{4}$ $2\frac{1}{4}$ _____

⑩ $2\frac{1}{3}$ $1\frac{2}{3}$ $2\frac{2}{3}$ _____

Find the sums or differences. Then write the answers in simplest form.

⑪ $\frac{3}{10} + \frac{9}{10} =$ _____ = _____

⑫ $\frac{11}{20} - \frac{7}{20} =$ _____ = _____

⑬ $\frac{6}{7} + \frac{6}{7} =$ _____ = _____

⑭ $\frac{2}{3} + \frac{2}{3} =$ _____ = _____

⑮ $\frac{8}{15} - \frac{2}{15} =$ _____ = _____

⑯ $\frac{7}{8} - \frac{1}{8} =$ _____ = _____

⑰ $\frac{11}{12} + \frac{5}{12} =$ _____ = _____

⑱ $\frac{5}{9} + \frac{4}{9} =$ _____ = _____

⑲ $\frac{15}{16} - \frac{7}{16} =$ _____ = _____

⑳ $\frac{5}{6} - \frac{1}{6} =$ _____ = _____

④ $9 \overline{)70.92}$

⑤ $5 \overline{)40.8}$

⑥ $3 \overline{)17.07}$

Complete the factor trees and write each number as a product of prime factors.

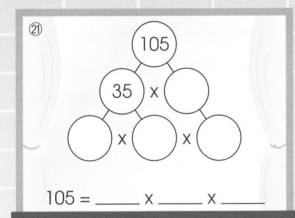

㉑

105 = _____ x _____ x _____

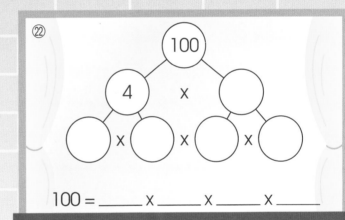

㉒

100 = _____ x _____ x _____ x _____

Calculate.

㉓	㉔	㉕
326 459 + 188	409 x 63	10 263 – 7 759
㉖ 15 x 9 + 23 =	㉗ 88 ÷ 2 – 7 =	㉘ 150 ÷ 5 + 4 =
㉙ 8 + 64 ÷ 4 =	㉚ 70 – 35 ÷ 7 =	㉛ 16 + 8 x 2 =

Find the volume of each solid. Then answer the questions.

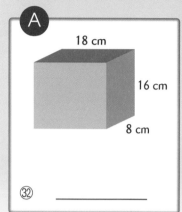

A

18 cm
16 cm
8 cm

㉜ _____

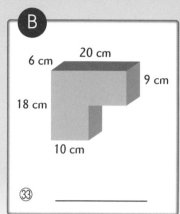

B

6 cm
20 cm
9 cm
18 cm
10 cm

㉝ _____

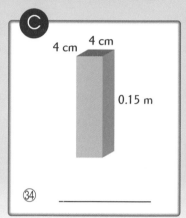

C

4 cm   4 cm
0.15 m

㉞ _____

㉟ Which solid has the greatest volume? _____

㊱ If Ⓐ weighs 250 g, what is the total mass of 8 Ⓐ in kg? _____ kg

㊲ 15 Ⓒ weigh 3 kg. How many grams does each Ⓒ weigh? _____ g

Solve the problems.

㊳ Joe has 46 stickers. If he buys 3 packs of stickers each containing 16 stickers, how many stickers will he have in all?

㊴ Each pack of stickers costs $4.95. How much do 3 packs of stickers cost?

See how many coloured pencils Helen has. Help her complete the table and use a circle graph to show the information. Then answer the questions.

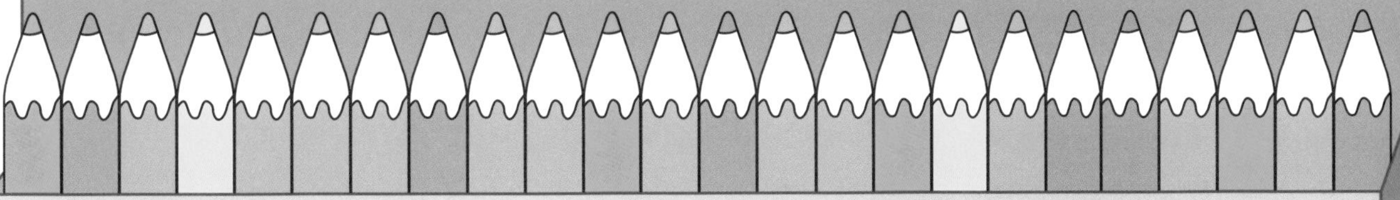

㊵

Colour	Red	Blue	Yellow	Purple
Number of Coloured Pencils				
Fraction of the whole (in simplest form)				

㊶ Coloured Pencils

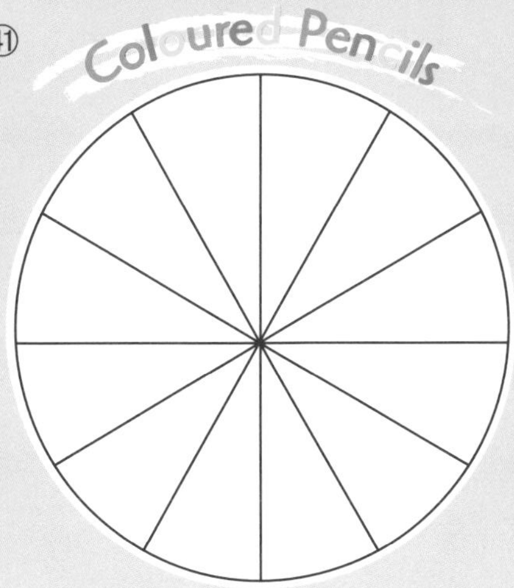

㊷ How many pencils does each sector in the circle graph represent?

_____ pencils

㊸ If each pencil costs 25¢, how much do the purple pencils cost?

$ _____

Look at the above circle graph. Then answer the questions.

㊹ If Helen lets her sister pick one pencil from her box of coloured pencils, what is the probability of picking

a. a red pencil? _____   b. a yellow pencil? _____

c. a blue pencil? _____   d. a purple pencil? _____

㊺ Is it more likely to pick a red pencil or a yellow pencil? _____

㊻ What is the probability of picking a green pencil? _____

Math – REVIEW

Write ordered pairs to represent each of the points on the grid. Then answer the questions.

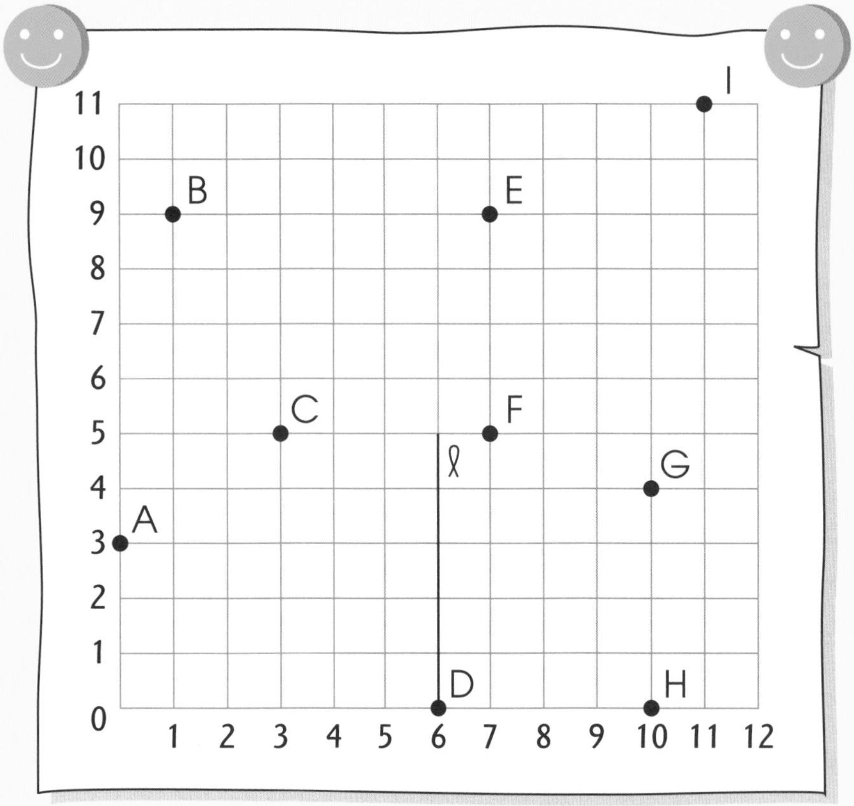

㊼ A ____________

B ____________

C ____________

D ____________

E ____________

F ____________

G ____________

H ____________

I ____________

㊽ Which points are horizontally 7 units from the origin? ____________

㊾ Join B, C, F, and E. What shape is BCFE? ____________

㊿ Which point should be translated so that BCFE will form a rectangle? How do you translate that point?

____

(51) Join D, H, and G. What shape is DHG?

____

(52) Reflect DHG over ℓ. What are the ordered pairs of the reflected DHG?

____

(53) Rotate DHG a quarter turn clockwise about G. What are the ordered pairs of the rotated DHG?

____

The data in the table follow a pattern. Complete the table and answer the questions.

54 The number of visitors:

a.

Date	Aug 16	Aug 18	Aug 20	Aug 22	Aug 24	Aug 26
No. of Visitors	250	400	700	1300		

b. On which day will the number of visitors be 9700? _____

c. How many visitors will there be on the first day of September? _____

Find the rates or ratios.

55 5 tickets for $21

$ _____ /ticket

56 run 720 m in 2 min

_____ m/min

57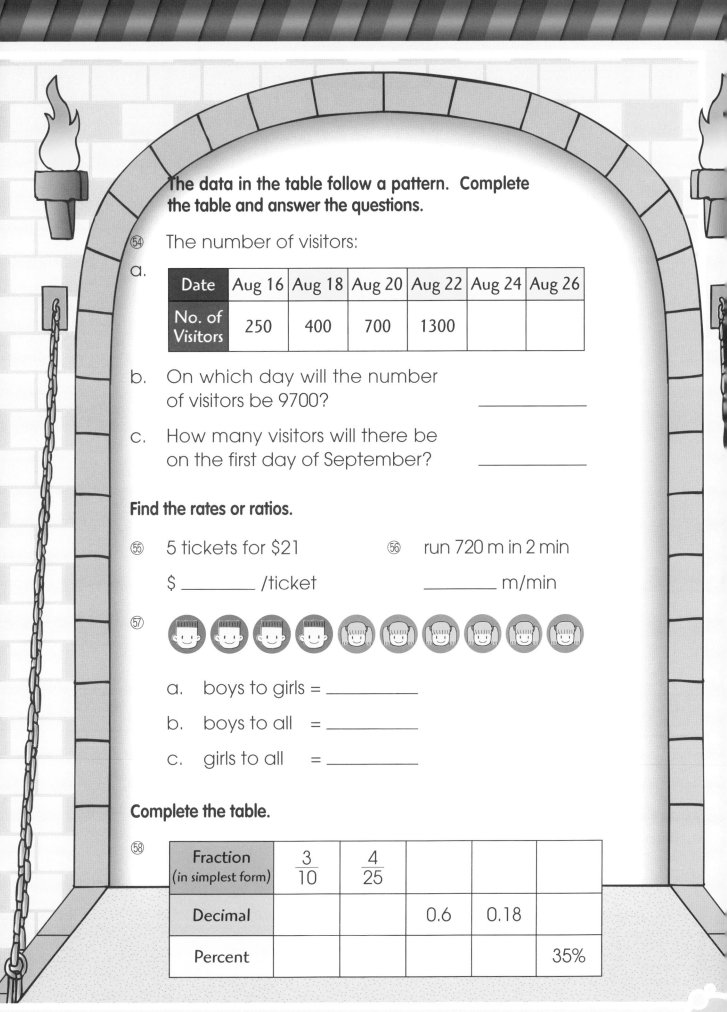

a. boys to girls = _____

b. boys to all   = _____

c. girls to all   = _____

Complete the table.

58

Fraction (in simplest form)	$\frac{3}{10}$	$\frac{4}{25}$			
Decimal			0.6	0.18	
Percent					35%

English

1 ASTEROIDS

Much speculation has been made of the possibility of an asteroid colliding with earth and Hollywood has profited handsomely from movies depicting such a <u>catastrophe</u>. Today, scientists are studying the probability of such a collision and the possibility of <u>deflecting</u> an asteroid heading towards earth. Asteroid fragments that have struck earth provide samples for scientists to study. Many scientists attribute changes to the earth's geography and the <u>extinction</u> of dinosaurs to asteroids that crashed into the earth millions of years ago.

Asteroids are formed from material left after the <u>formation</u> of the solar system approximately 4.5 billion years ago. Most asteroids <u>orbit</u> the sun between Jupiter and Mars. This asteroid <u>region</u> is called the Main Belt and contains millions of asteroids of varying sizes. The largest is Ceres which is 940 km in diameter.

Asteroids were first spotted by telescope in 1801. In 1991 the NASA spacecraft, Galileo, was the first to <u>observe</u> an asteroid using the fly-by method. In 2001 NASA landed a spacecraft on the asteroid Eros and was able to do <u>extensive</u> scientific <u>research</u>.

Recent research tells us that there is little <u>likelihood</u> of a NEO (Near Earth Object) striking earth. In fact, <u>statistics</u> suggest that a NEO strikes earth once or twice every million years. If one did strike, it would destroy a <u>fraction</u> of the earth and kill a portion of the earth's population.

Fortunately, unlike most natural disasters, a collision with an asteroid may be <u>avoidable</u>. In the scientific <u>community</u> it is believed that an asteroid would pass near earth many times before striking. This should give enough warning time to plan to deflect the asteroid from its path. The key to protecting ourselves, though, is not so much in the defence upon the threat of a collision, but in the finding of the asteroids heading our way in time to plan a defence <u>strategy</u>.

A. **Select the best answer to complete the statements below.**

1. The first telescope spotting of asteroids occurred in _____ .

   A. 1901   B. 1801   C. 1701

2. NEO stands for _____ .

   A. No Entry into Orbit   B. No Earth Orbit   C. Near Earth Object

3. The solar system may have been formed as long as _____ .

   A. 4.5 billion years ago   B. 10 billion years ago
   C. 5 million years ago

4. The Galileo spacecraft was the first to observe an asteroid using a _____ .

   A. surveillance system   B. fly-by method   C. high-powered lense

5. Scientists believe that before an asteroid strikes, there will be _____ .

   A. short warning   B. no warning
   C. enough warning to plan a defence

6. The main defence against an asteroid would be _____ .

   A. blowing it up   B. changing the earth's orbit
   C. deflecting it

7. Asteroids have been credited with _____ .

   A. the extinction of dinosaurs   B. changes to the geography of the earth
   C. both A and B

8. Most asteroids orbit the sun between _____ .

   A. Saturn and Venus   B. the earth and its moon
   C. Jupiter and Mars

9. Most asteroids are found in the _____ .

   A. Milky Way   B. Main Belt   C. Asteroid Belt

10. Scientists believe an asteroid strikes earth once or twice every _____ .

    A. million years   B. billion years   C. 10,000 years

B. **Enter each of the underlined words in the reading passage to match the definition or synonym given.**

Paragraph 1

1. [_____] no longer exists

2. [_____] terrible event, disaster

3. [_____] to force to change direction

Paragraph 2

4. [_____] go around regularly

5. [_____] specific area, location, or place

6. [_____] creation, building, construction

Paragraph 3

7. [_____] a great deal, very thorough

8. [_____] study, investigation

9. [_____] watch closely

Paragraph 4

10. [_____] numbers, figures used to create facts

11. [_____] probability, chance

12. [_____] a mathematical portion of a whole thing

Paragraph 5

13. [_____] people with common interests, a group

14. [_____] carefully thought-out plan of action

15. [_____] able to evade, to get away from something

Adjectives and Adverbs

An **adjective** describes a noun. An **adverb** describes a verb. Adverbs often answer the questions: where, when, how.

C.   Identify the adjectives and adverbs in the following sentences.

1.   Numerous asteroids are clearly visible through small telescopes.

adjective : _____   adverb : _____

2.   High-speed asteroids that are frequently directed at earth are called meteoroids.

adjective : _____   adverb : _____

3.   The tremendous heat of a speeding meteoroid causes it to eventually break into small pieces.

adjective : _____   adverb : _____

4.   We scientifically refer to these smaller pieces as meteorites.

adjective : _____   adverb : _____

5.   Stony meteorites are extremely difficult to identify because they look like ordinary rocks.

adjective : _____

adverb   : _____

There may be more than one adjective in a sentence.

6.   Our naked eye can barely spot huge asteroids.

adjective : _____

adverb   : _____

2 The World's Most Famous Doll

It is difficult to believe that this year (2004) Barbie, the most famous doll in the world, turns 45. Her slim figure, striking good looks, and fashionable clothes continue to make Barbie an American fashion and lifestyle icon.

Barbie was the invention of Ruth and Elliot Handler, founders of Mattel Toys, who named the doll after their daughter. Ruth had observed her daughter playing with paper dolls and verbalizing adult-like conversation between these dolls. She decided then to create a three-dimensional representation of a doll that would symbolize the American ideal of what a young woman should be like. After much research and design, Ruth Handler unveiled this teenage fashion doll at New York Toy Fair in 1959.

The next evolutionary step in the development of Barbie as we know her today was to establish a clothing line. Handler commissioned Charlotte Johnson to be in charge of the Barbie clothing line. By 1961 the Barbie craze had spread to Europe. That same year Ken, Barbie's boyfriend, came on the scene. In 1964 "college" Barbie was introduced and became the epitome of the modern woman – educated and sophisticated. Barbie then evolved into a modern, professional woman assuming over 80 careers, including doctor, rock star, astronaut, and presidential candidate. The first black Barbie was introduced in 1980, and in an effort to establish worldwide appeal, Barbie underwent design changes to represent over 40 different nationalities.

The first Barbie was sold for $3, with 350,000 dolls purchased that year in the US. That same doll, the 1959 version, would fetch over $10,000 today at an auction. The Barbie business generates an estimated 1.5 billion dollars annually with roughly two dolls purchased every second somewhere in the world.

Millions of children visit the Barbie website (www.barbie.com) where they can peruse the latest fashions, join the Barbie fan club, and purchase accessories. Even as Barbie heads towards middle age, the fascination with this symbol of perfection continues to grow.

A. Put a checkmark ✔ beside the statement that best identifies the main idea of each paragraph from the reading passage.

Paragraph 1

1. _____ Barbie is fashionable.

2. _____ Barbie is the most famous doll in the world.

3. _____ Barbie has been around for a long time.

Paragraph 2

1. _____ Barbie symbolized an ideal young person in America.

2. _____ Ruth Handler invented Barbie after watching her daughter play with dolls.

3. _____ Ruth and Elliot Handler were the founders of Mattel Toys.

Paragraph 3

1. _____ Barbie dolls evolved over the years.

2. _____ Ken was Barbie's boyfriend.

3. _____ There was a "college" Barbie doll.

Paragraph 4

1. _____ Barbie dolls generate a lot of money.

2. _____ Barbie dolls are too expensive.

3. _____ Kids are always buying Barbie dolls.

Paragraph 5

1. _____ Barbie is still popular with children today.

2. _____ Barbie continues to get old.

3. _____ Barbie is on the Internet.

B. Answer the questions by recalling the details.

1. Where and when was the first Barbie revealed to the public?

    At _____ in _____

2. What was the retail cost of the first Barbie? How much would that first doll be worth today?

    $ _____ and $ _____

3. How many different career-type Barbies have been created?

    _____

4. What year did Barbie meet her boyfriend Ken?

    _____

5. How many nationalities has Barbie been redesigned to represent?

    _____

The Complete Sentence

A **complete sentence** contains a subject (or an understood subject) and a verb. It also conveys a complete thought. An **incomplete sentence** is called a fragment.

C. Write F (fragment) or C (complete) beside each entry below.

1. Barbie who is getting older.

2. If you placed, head to toe, all the Barbie dolls and family members sold since 1959, they would circle the earth seven times.

3. Midge, Barbie's best friend doll, was introduced in 1959.

4. A Barbie represented a candidate for president of the US in 1992.

5. Skipper, Tutti, Stacie, Kelly, and Krissy, the five sisters of Barbie.

6. Dolls are the second most popular items to collect in the US behind stamps.

7. The US army approved the costumes of Military Barbie.

8. The Ken doll was named after the son of the founders of Mattel.

Adjective and Adverb Phrases

Adjective and **adverb phrases** are groups of words that describe nouns and verbs. These phrases are introduced by prepositions.

Examples: in the house, over the hill, under the carpet, beside the desk

D. **Place parentheses ( ) around the phrases in each sentence below.**

1. Twiggy, the famous fashion model, was the first of the celebrity Barbies.

2. Ruth Handler was one of the creators of Barbie in 1959.

3. In 1964 Barbie went to college, but she would have been only five years of age.

4. The bendable legs of Barbie were not introduced until 1965.

5. Barbie was in the Olympics and competed against an Olympic swimmer.

6. The sale of Barbie is common in more than 150 countries around the world.

7. The best-selling Barbie of all time was "Totally Hair" Barbie.

8. The hair on "Totally Hair" Barbie stretched from head to toe.

9. In the year 1999 Barbie skated with in-line skates.

10. There are over 100 new outfits added to Barbie's wardrobe every year.

61

3 Shopping Malls.

On weekends across Canada, many young people <u>flock</u> to the malls to <u>browse</u>, shop, or meet friends. Shopping malls also offer shelter from the extreme cold of the Canadian winter or relief from the <u>insufferable</u> heat of summer. Senior citizens like meeting in malls for "mall walks", a modern day fitness activity for those in need of <u>ideal</u> conditions for exercise.

Malls are not a modern <u>phenomenon</u>. In fact, the early mall concept goes back to medieval Europe where shoppers made their weekly purchases in piazzas or agoras. The Galleria Victor Emmanuel of Milan was the first fully-enclosed shopping mall. Advancement in transportation encouraged the widespread development of suburbs, and <u>consequently</u>, malls <u>sprouted up</u> in these areas. By the late 1890's, "store blocks" were developed resembling the "strip mall" <u>common</u> today. Central to the growth of the mall was the automobile. Once people became mobile, they were free to travel to newly-developed shopping centres where parking was <u>plentiful</u> and the stores were diverse.

The three largest shopping centres in the world are the West Edmonton Mall in Edmonton, Alberta, the Mall of Arabia in Dubai, United Arab Emirates, and the Mall of America in Bloomington, Minnesota. The largest, the West Edmonton Mall, is not just a shopping centre; it is a huge entertainment centre featuring seven world class attractions. The mall features the world's largest indoor amusement park, the world's largest wave pool, and the world's largest indoor lake offering submarine rides. There is also a mini golf centre, a professional-sized skating rink, a dolphin lagoon, and Sea Life Caverns – home to 200 species of marine life. Rounding out the vast entertainment <u>spectrum</u> is a Las Vegas-styled casino, nightclubs, a Playdium, and a 3-D Imax theatre.

The days of supremacy will soon come to a close for the West Edmonton Mall. Dubai is planning the construction of an 810,000-square metre mall (approximately the size of 50 soccer fields) that will cater to an expected 3.2 billion shoppers.

Fact or Opinion

A **fact** can be proven by referring to the text. An **opinion** is an interpretation of information such as a person's thoughts or feelings about a subject.

A. **Refer to the reading passage and place "F" for fact or "O" for opinion beside each statement below.**

1. The West Edmonton Mall is one of the largest shopping centres in the world. _____

2. Shopping malls are popular places. _____

3. Shopping malls are meant for people with cars. _____

4. The first malls were called "store blocks". _____

5. Canadians go to malls for reasons other than shopping. _____

6. The growing use of the automobile helped the growth of malls. _____

7. The root of the mall concept goes back to medieval Europe. _____

8. The first fully-enclosed shopping mall was the Galleria Victor Emmanuel of Milan. _____

9. Shopping malls are too busy and do not have adequate parking. _____

10. There are many interesting stores in shopping malls. _____

11. The West Edmonton Mall is also a huge entertainment complex. _____

12. The world's largest indoor lake is found in the West Edmonton Mall. _____

Your Opinion

Give reasons for your answer.

Do you think that malls will become bigger and better in the future or do you think they will become extinct?

_____

_____

_____

Independent and Dependent Clauses

Like a sentence, an **independent clause** has a subject and a verb. A **dependent clause** also has a subject and a verb but begins with a subordinating word, which makes it dependent on more information.

B. Underline the dependent clause and place parentheses ( ) around the independent clause in each sentence below.

If the dependent clause appears first, it is separated from the independent clause by a comma.

1. After watching the movie, they went for a bite to eat.

2. Because it started to rain, the race was cancelled.

3. If his team win this game, they win the championship.

4. She invited her friends to her house before they left for the party.

5. It snowed heavily while they were driving home.

6. Whenever they met, they had a long chat.

C. Form a sentence by making one of the two clauses dependent.

Add subordinating words such as after, while, before, during, whenever, if, because, when...

1. the circus came to town   they were absent from school

_____

2. he invited his friends over   they played cards

_____

3. the students were quiet

the teacher asked for everyone's attention

_____

4. she forgot her books at school   she will not be able to do her homework

_____

5. it became difficult to see   the fog rolled in

_____

6. the car broke down

they were stranded on the highway

_____

D. Cross out X the bolded words in the passage below and replace them with synonyms. Use the underlined words in the reading passage.

Steven and Michael enjoy going to the mall and **looking** in the various stores. The choices of stores are **numerous**, but to end up in clothing stores is a **normal** occurrence for them. **As a result**, the **perfect** situation of not spending money becomes a **rarity**. In the summer many of their friends avoid the **unbearable** temperatures outside by heading to the local malls. Since many new malls have **appeared** close by, they have a choice of places to gather. In the larger malls, the **collection** of shops is overwhelming so they only visit a few of their favourites.

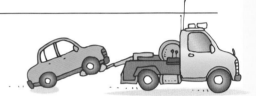

4 SKATEBOARDING

All across Canada, on residential streets, at office tower concourses, and just about anywhere where a step or railing can be found, you will find them – skateboarders. They are a special breed of athletes. Skateboarders compete fiercely to accomplish designed feats of skill, yet they also support one another. When a skater accomplishes an "ollie" (hands-free jump) or any difficult manoeuvre, skater buddies will applaud the effort and appreciate that a new standard has been set for them to reach. Skaters are very focused and intent upon improving their skills and challenging themselves to new heights of performance.

Although skateboarding has been steadily growing in popularity, it is by no means a new sport. The first evidence of skateboarding dates back to the early 1900's when skateboards consisted of roller-skate wheels attached to a 2-by-4 plank of wood. Some of these resembled scooters since they had handles attached for balance. It wasn't until the 1950's that the first Roller Derby brand skateboard was available. At this point skateboarding was still a relatively new sport. It didn't become a mainstream sport until a surfing magazine in California began to feature it. Skateboarding was an obvious "street" transition of surfing. In 1963 a company named Makaha produced the first professional skateboard and assembled a team to promote the product to the public.

After brisk sales of skateboards in the early 1960's, skateboarding became almost non-existent. Manufacturers were so intent on mass producing skateboards that they failed to do adequate research and development to improve the safety of the product. Consequently, skaters were getting injured regularly. Fatal accidents, frequent serious injuries, and a dislike of the sport by the general public, forced cities to ban the activity. However, with the invention of urethane wheels, safety and performance improved and the evolution of skateboarding resumed steadily over the next thirty years.

Today there are skate parks, televised professional competitions, sophisticated equipment, trade publications, and specialized clothing. On any city street, you will find a small gathering of local skaters, often jumping off homemade ramps, in friendly competition for the perfect "ollie" or the best "kicktail".

Skimming to Find Answers

Skimming for information involves reading through material quickly, looking for key words related to the question you are trying to answer.

A.   Answer the following questions.

1. What is an "**ollie**"?

    _____

2. In the early **1900's** what did skateboards consist of?

    _____

3. How do "**skater buddies**" support one another?

    _____

4. Which company produced the first **professional** skateboard?

    _____

5. Give three reasons that skateboarding was **banned** in some cities.

    _____

6. Why was the invention of **urethane** wheels important?

    _____

7. Where do **city skateboarders** like to practise?

    _____

8. What helped skateboarding become a **mainstream** sport?

    _____

9. How are skateboarders competitive in the **best way**?

    _____

10. In what way did early skateboards resemble **scooters**?

    _____

Compound Sentences

A **compound sentence** has two independent clauses (simple sentences) joined by a conjunction (and, or, but).

B. **Use the appropriate conjunctions to join the following pairs of sentences.**

1. Is it better to mind your own business?
   Is it appropriate to speak your mind?

   _____

2. The boys played baseball in the schoolyard.
   The bell rang and they were called back to class.

   _____

3. Students were called to an assembly in the gymnasium.
   The principal spoke to them about safety.

   _____

4. She invited everyone to her birthday party.
   Not everyone was able to show up.

   _____

Compound-Complex Sentences

A **compound-complex sentence** has two independent clauses (sentences) joined by a conjunction with at least one dependent clause.

Challenge

Use each group of three statements to form a compound-complex sentence.

1. The wind was blowing fiercely.
   The sailboat dipped and swayed.
   The waves crashed against the bow.

   _____

   _____

   _____

2. The grade six students put on a school play.
   The gymnasium was filled with spectators.
   Everyone enjoyed the performances.

   _____

   _____

   _____

Word Derivatives

A **derivative** is another form of the same word.

Example: the word "recall" is a derivative of the word "call".

To form new words you can add suffixes (able, ance, ence, ful, less, ation, ition, er, ity...) or prefixes (de, re, a, anti, in...) to an existing word.

C. **Give a derivative word that fits in each sentence below. The first one is done for you.**

1. The puppy was cute and <u>lovable</u>.   (love)

2. The skateboarders were _____ when riding the railing.   (care)

3. Down the street went the skateboards in perfect _____ .   (form)

4. There was special parking available for _____ people.   (able)

5. Because there was a _____ , they were able to get tickets. (cancel)

6. Because the skaters were so good, the contest was very _____ . (compete)

7. The skater was disappointed because he was _____ to match the "ollie" of his competitor.   (able)

8. The relatives arrived _____ in the middle of the night.   (expect)

5 The Canadian Comedy Icon

YEAH, baby

If you told Mike Myers's classmates from his high school graduating class of 1982 that by 2003 he would be honoured as a member of the Canadian Walk of Fame and one of the best known and loved film comedians in the world, they would have probably laughed. With a reported compensation of $25,000,000 for the third Austin Powers movie, Myers is also one of the highest-paid actors.

But how did a funny kid from a working-class Scarborough home reach such a pinnacle of fame? Much of Mike Myers's inspiration came from his family. His mother had been an aspiring actress and his father loved comedy, particularly British humour. His parents came to Canada from Liverpool, England, and in recognition of his ancestry, Myers holds a British passport today. As a youth Myers loved to entertain and create characters at parties. On the day he wrote his final high school exam, he auditioned for a spot in Second City, a comedy club in Toronto. It was there that Martin Short, then of Saturday Night Live, saw him perform and arranged an audition with Saturday Night Live. Myers developed a number of memorable characters including his famous character Wayne Deiter. He then went on to write and star in the film Wayne's World for which he was paid $1,000,000. In 1991 his father died of Alzheimer's disease and his brother was killed in a car accident. Myers decided to take a break from performing and took a year off, but in 1993, he was back starring in Wayne's World II.

Myers developed his greatest character as a spin-off combination of The Pink Panther's inspector Clouseau, detective Matt Helm, and internationally famous spy, James Bond. Austin Powers became the character that complemented all his talents: his love of British humour, his ability to create characters, and his creativity as a writer. The phrases "Oh, beeeHAVE" and "YEAH, baby" became the trademark of Powers – fashion photographer by day, international spy by night.

Although internationally famous, Mike Myers has been a faithful supporter of Toronto acting as an ambassador for Toronto during the SARS outbreak. In recognition of his Toronto roots, a street in Scarborough, Mike Myers Drive, was so named in his honour.

A. **Mark "T" for true or "F" for false in the circle following each statement.**

1. Mike Myers was paid $25,000,000 for the third Austin Powers film. ◯

2. Mike Myers was born in Ottawa. ◯

3. Mike Myers has a shopping mall named after him. ◯

4. Myers's parents came from Ireland. ◯

5. Wayne Deiter was Myers's close friend. ◯

6. Myers took a year off before making Wayne's World II. ◯

7. In 2003 Myers was entered into the Canadian Walk of Fame. ◯

8. Myers holds only a Canadian passport. ◯

9. Myers auditioned for Second City after finishing university. ◯

10. Comedian Martin Short arranged an audition for Myers. ◯

11. Myers starred in Wayne's World but he did not write it. ◯

12. Myers was paid $500,000 for the first Wayne's World film. ◯

B. **Give a short, factual answer for each question below.**

1. Where did Mike Myers get his inspiration to become a comedian?

_____

2. How was the Austin Powers character created?

_____

3. What did Myers often do with his friends at parties?

_____

Verbals

Verbals are forms of a verb that do not act as a verb in a sentence. Verbals can be nouns, adjectives, or adverbs.

C. Use each of the following verbals in a sentence. Make the verbal the subject of the sentence.

When a verbal ends in "ing" and is used as a noun, it is called a **gerund**.
Example: **Eating** vegetables is good for you.

1. skipping : _____

2. skiing : _____

3. laughing : _____

4. talking : _____

5. playing : _____

D. Use each of the following participles in a sentence.

Participles are verbals used as adjectives.
Example: He wore a red **hunting** jacket so he would be visible.

1. blowing : _____

2. floating : _____

3. singing : _____

4. shopping : _____

5. running : _____

E. Use each of the following infinitives in a sentence.

An **infinitive** is the "to" form of the verb. It can be a noun, an adjective, or an adverb in a sentence.
Example: **To read** a good book gives her great pleasure.

1. to remember : _____

2. to run : _____

3. to drive   : _____

4. to listen : _____

5. to watch : _____

Root Words

A **root word** is the part of the word that contains its basic meaning. Many of our words are derived from Latin root words.

F. **For each Latin root word, create 2 new words. The basic word meaning is given in parentheses.**

Example: capt (seize)	capture	captivate
1. scrib (write)	trans_____	in_____
2. port (carry)	trans_____	im_____
3. mit (send)	sub_____	re_____
4. stat (stand)	sta_____	sta_____
5. cred (believe)	in_____	cr_____
6. vers (turn)	re_____	con_____

Challenge

Refer to the above Latin roots. Give a definition for the italicized word in each of the following sentences.

1.   His *portable* radio fit neatly into his pocket.

_____

2.   The *transmission* of the information was quick.

_____

3.   He lost his *credibility* when he told a lie.

_____

6

The Building of Disneyland

Walt Disney, the famous cartoonist that created the Disney Empire, had a dream of creating a magical place where children and their parents could experience the fantasy world of Disney. Before construction of the "Magic Kingdom", as it was to be called, could begin, three problems had to be solved: what the park would consist of, where it would be built, and how to pay for it.

Initially, Walt Disney thought that 8 acres would suffice. Walt had time to reconsider this plan because in 1941 World War II broke out and his plans were put on hold. By 1953 Disney realized that he would need at least 100 acres to construct his dream park. The financiers from whom Disney hoped to get the money to build the park were not as enthusiastic about the idea, so Disney turned to his TV show "Disneyland" to promote the project. He purchased a 160-acre site in Orange County, California and in 1953 construction began.

His idea was to build five areas within the park. Main Street would offer a revival of the small town American ideal; Adventureland would take the visitors to the exotic lands of Asia and Africa; Frontierland would offer a glimpse of the pioneer days of American history; Fantasyland, which features a Sleeping Beauty castle and a fantasy village, would be the place where "dreams would come true"; Tomorrowland would offer a look at the future. The cost of the "Magic Kingdom" began at 9 million dollars and swelled to 17 million before it opened on July 17, 1955 after two years of construction.

Opening day was not without its problems. Local residents protested the park, considering it a neighbourhood disturbance. A strike by plumbers created a drinking water shortage so few fountains were available. The temperature on opening day was an unbearable 38°C and the asphalt on the walkways was melting, trapping the pointy heals of ladies' shoes. Nearly 30,000 counterfeit tickets were discovered to have been used at the gates. Nevertheless, the "Magic Kingdom" became a reality. At the age of 53, Walt Disney fulfilled his dream.

After only two years, Disneyland was profitable. From 1955 to 1965, 50 million visitors passed through the gates. Today, Disney Inc. includes parks in Tokyo, Paris, and Orlando, a cruise line in the Bahamas, and a film and television empire.

A. Read the passage and answer the questions.

1. Why did Disney want to create the "Magic Kingdom"?

   _____

   _____

2. Before building the "Magic Kingdom", what three problems had to be solved?

   _____

   _____

3. What important event in 1941 delayed Disney's building plans?

   _____

   _____

4. How many acres did Disney initially think he would need for the Kingdom and how many did he actually purchase?

   _____

   _____

5. How did Disney promote the "Magic Kingdom" project when he was having trouble finding money to fund it?

   _____

   _____

6. Name the five areas or lands of the "Magic Kingdom".

   _____

   _____

7. How many years did it take to build the "Magic Kingdom" and at what final cost?

   _____

   _____

8. Describe the four major problems on opening day.

   _____

   _____

Subject-Verb Agreement

A verb and a subject must agree in number.

Examples: She **has**   Susie **walks**   (singular)
           We **have**   They **have**   Mark and John **walk**   (plural)

B.   Select the correct verb to match the subject of each sentence below. Write it in the blank.

1.   The number of students in the class (is, are) _____ larger than expected.

2.   The effort of the players (surprise, surprises) _____ the coach.

3.   Each product (appear, appears) _____ to be the best.

4.   The clothes in the dryer (is, are) _____ still wet.

5.   The marching band (entertains, entertain) _____ at the football game.

6.   The discussion of politics (are, is) _____ part of history class.

7.   The computer programs (is, are) _____ expensive.

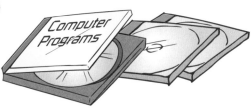

8.   The doughnuts in the box (was, were) _____ stale.

Compound Subjects

Compound subjects are treated as plural.
Example: Paul and Jim play on the same team.

If the parts of a compound subject are joined by "or" or "nor", the verb should agree with the closest subject.
Example: Neither the bus driver nor the passengers enjoy the trip.

C.   Select the correct verb to match the subject of each sentence below. Write it in the blank.

1.   Randall, Kara, and Lauren (goes, go) _____ snowboarding on weekends.

2.   The cats and dogs actually (plays, play) _____ together happily.

3.   Either Paul or Phil (are, is) _____ a good choice for class representative.

4. Neither one of the cars (start, starts) _____ in the cold.

5. The student and her friends (walk, walks) _____ home.

6. Either Joseph or his brothers (are, is) _____ doing the yard work.

7. The shirt and the pants (matches, match) _____ .

8. Neither the teacher nor her students (enjoy, enjoys) _____ the presentation.

Homonyms

Homonyms are words that sound alike but are not related in meaning.
Examples: vary, very; bow, bough; way, weigh

D.   Use the two clues to find the homonym pairs.

1. boundaries of a country   b ____ ____ d ____ r

   person who pays for food and lodgings   b ____ a ____ d e ____

2. a bright colour   r ____ ____

   what you did with a book   r ____ a ____

   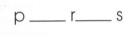

3. holes in the skin   p ____ r ____ s

   empty liquid   p ____ ____ r ____

4. found below the knees   ____ e ____ t

   an amazing act   f ____ ____ t

   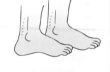

5. fuzzy leather   ____ u e ____ e

   moved back and forth   s w ____ ____ e d

6. a lowered price   ____ a l ____

   travel on a boat   ____ ____ i ____

7. listen   ____ e a ____

   not there but   ____ e r ____

8. a dog's feet   ____ ____ w s

   stop for a moment   ____ a u ____ e

7 Earthquakes

Earthquakes can be nature's most devastating phenomenon. Most earthquakes are relatively harmless, but every so often, an earthquake occurs which results in huge casualties and property damage. The deadliest earthquake in history occurred in China in 1556 when 830,000 people were killed. The worst earthquake in the twentieth century occurred in Tsangun, China where 255,000 people lost their lives. The largest, however, was the Chilean earthquake in 1960 which measured an unsurpassed 9.5 on the Richter scale.

Earthquakes are a result of stress within the earth which bends the earth's crustal plates. These plates eventually split causing "faults" that are followed by vibrations of varying degree. It is these vibrations that we call earthquakes. The English professors John Milne, Thomas Gray, and James Ewing are credited with developing the first seismic instruments (seismographs) sensitive enough to be used to study earthquakes. The inspiration for seismology (the study of earthquake activity) began in 1775 after 70,000 people in Portugal were killed and the city of Lisbon was ruined. Charles Richter, an American, invented the Richter scale which measures the actual power of an earthquake. The higher the reading, the more powerful and potentially dangerous the earthquake. For example, a reading of 6.0 on the Richter scale is 10 times as powerful as a reading of 5.0.

The 1906 San Francisco earthquake brought the San Andreas Fault to the attention of American seismologists. Here the Pacific Plate on the west moved opposite to the American Plate on the east causing a fault 1,300 kilometres long and 16 kilometres deep into the earth. While a major earthquake in this area is likely, it will not occur without warning.

In Canada there are roughly 1,500 earthquakes reported annually, but only 100 of these reach a Richter reading of 3 and would be felt by human beings. An earthquake must have a reading of 6 or greater to cause significant damage. The strongest earthquake in Canada occurred in 1949 off the coast of Queen Charlotte Islands, British Columbia, and measured 8.1.

A.   Circle the letter of the correct fact that completes each statement.

1. The first seismic instruments were developed by _____ .

    A. three American professors   B. three English professors

    C. three Portugese professors   D. three Canadian professors

2. On record the worst earthquake of the twentieth century in terms of lives lost occurred in _____ .

    A. California   B. China   C. Chile   D. South America

3. The largest earthquake recorded on the Richter scale was in _____ .

    A. Mexico   B. China   C. Chile   D. California

4. When the Pacific Plate moved opposite of the American Plate, it formed _____ .

    A. San Francisco   B. the American Fault

    C. the San Andreas Fault   D. the Pacific Fault

5. Each year, in Canada there are approximately _____ .

    A. 1,500 earthquakes   B. 50 earthquakes

    C. 15,000 earthquakes   D. 15 earthquakes

6. In the deadliest earthquake on record in 1556, the number of deaths was _____ .

    A. 530,000   B. 630,000   C. 830,000   D. 83,000

7. Canada's strongest earthquake measured _____ .

    A. 4.5   B. 7.1   C. 9.1   D. 8.1

8. Earthquakes are a result of _____ .

    A. stress within the earth   B. shifting plates

    C. bad weather   D. volcanoes

9. The scale for measuring the power of an earthquake was developed by _____ .

    A. James Ewing   B. Thomas Gray

    C. John Milne   D. Charles Richter

10. Canada's strongest earthquake occurred in _____ .

    A. British Columbia   B. Ontario

    C. Newfoundland   D. Manitoba

Correct Usage

Rules of use for verbs often confused:

- **bring** refers to movement toward; **take** refers to motion away.
- **lie** refers to resting in a flat position; **lay** means to place something .
- **let** means to allow; **leave** means to go away from somewhere.
- **may** asks for permission; **can** refers to ability to do something.
- **sit** means to use a seat; **set** means to place something.
- **rise** means to go upwards or ascend; **raise** means to lift up.

B. **State whether the usage in each of the following sentences is correct (C) or incorrect (INC).**

1. May I borrow your pencil? _____

2. Would you please take me my dinner? _____

3. You should bring this book to its owner. _____

4. Take their coats and put them in the closet. _____

5. Jason asked his boss for a rise. _____

6. I don't think I may go with you to the concert tomorrow. _____

7. Let the dog go out into the backyard. _____

8. Lay the blanket over the bed. _____

Usage Confusion

These pairs of words may cause usage confusion:

- **accept** means to agree to receive something; **except** means not to include.
- **among** is used when referring to more than two things; **between** is used when referring to only two things.
- **borrow** means to receive something as a loan; **lend** means to give something as a loan.
- **fewer** refers to a number of items; **less** refers to quantity.
- **in** means inside; **into** means to move from outside to inside.

C. **State whether the usage in each of the following sentences is correct (C) or incorrect (INC).**

1. The actor excepted the Academy Award. _____

2. They shared the pizza between the four friends. _____

3. I will lend the book from you if you don't mind. _____

4. She walked into the room and sat down. _____

5. Most of his friends were in his class. _____

6. Everyone went skating except him. _____

7. They kept a secret between the two of them. _____

8. Could you lend me your bicycle for the day? _____

Descriptive Language

We have five senses: tasting, smelling, hearing, seeing, and touching. Descriptive language that appeals to these senses makes descriptions more vivid and meaningful.

D.   Select and circle the most effective descriptive word for each of the following sentences.

1. They refused to swim in the _____ lake water.

   warm   murky   gentle   blue

2. She wore a _____ blue coat with her red hat.

   shiny   bright   completely

3. The _____ bird had a brightly-coloured beak.

   wild   large   exotic

4. The _____ cold wind howled through the bare trees.

   wet   freezing   damp

5. The _____ of garbage rose from the dump.

   aroma   stench   smell

6. The family enjoyed a _____ roast chicken dinner.

   hot   nice   succulent

7. The _____ peanut brittle stuck to his teeth.

   sweet   hard   crunchy

8. He heard the _____ coming from his leaky tire.

   hiss   noise   sound

8 Stephanie Dotto – Making a Difference

So often when we witness the <u>fate</u> of poor people in the world, we feel sad yet unable to do anything to help. Stephanie Dotto proved that one person can make a difference in the lives of so many.

Malawi is an <u>impoverished</u> third world country in central Africa. There, the infant mortality rate is 200 times greater than that in Canada. One in three working adults suffers from AIDS. The average life <u>expectancy</u> is only 37 years as opposed to Canada where life expectancy is one of the world's highest at 80 years. The average family earns the <u>equivalent</u> of $200 per year.

In 2000, massive flooding <u>devastated</u> Malawi. Barefooted children with open cuts waded through the polluted floodwaters becoming <u>infected</u>. When 16-year-old Stephanie Dotto, a high school student from Montreal, saw images of those poor children, she decided to do something about it. Like any high school student, Stephanie was busy doing projects for school. She teamed up with her friend, Jennifer Goehring, to make the suffering of the Malawi children their special project. Through <u>dedication</u> and hard work, they collected and shipped 1,000 pairs of shoes for the Malawi children.

Stephanie's next project involved raising funds for medical aid packages known as PTP's (Physicians Travel Packages). Each PTP contains vaccines and medical supplies and can help up to 1,500 people; however, the medicine in each PTP unit costs approximately $6,000 with preparation costs in the range of $500 per unit. Stephanie attempts to <u>overcome</u> this expense by appealing to <u>corporations</u> for sponsorship. She has teamed up with Pharmahorizons, a medical service group, to achieve her goal of bringing medical aid to the needy in Malawi.

In the future, Stephanie intends to complete a nursing degree and use her <u>expertise</u> to help the ill in places like Malawi.

A. **Read the passage and fill in the blanks with numerical answers.**

1. Each PTP (Physicians Travel Package) can provide aid for _____ people.

2. Life expectancy in Canada is _____ years.

3. The infant mortality rate in Malawi is _____ times greater than that in Canada.

4. Massive floods devastated Malawi in the year _____ .

5. Stephanie and Jennifer collected _____ pairs of shoes.

6. The life expectancy in Malawi is _____ years.

7. The average family in Malawi earns $ _____ per year.

8. The cost of a PTP is approximately $ _____ .

9. It costs $ _____ to prepare a PTP.

10. In Malawi, one in _____ adults suffers from AIDS.

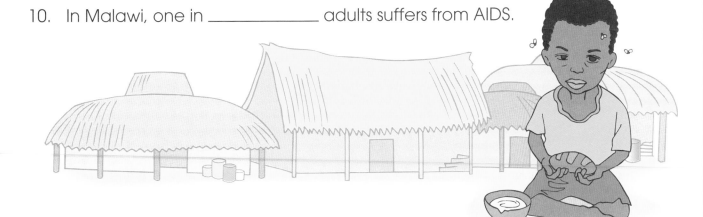

B. **Answer the following questions, using facts to form opinions.**

1. How would you describe Stephanie's character?

   _____

2. What does this reading passage teach us about helping others?

   _____

3. Is a nursing career a good choice for Stephanie? Explain.

   _____

C. For each underlined word from the reading passage listed below, circle the best synonym based on the meaning of the word as used in the passage.

1. fate	future	past	destiny	hope
2. impoverished	unhappy	poor	enriched	improved
3. expectancy	time	history	duration	location
4. equivalent	balance	equal	amount	total
5. devastated	ruined	designed	damaged	hurt
6. infected	injured	sickened	invaded	diseased
7. dedication	celebration	intelligence	devotion	duty
8. overcome	endure	defeat	satisfy	meet
9. corporations	dynasties	businesses	authorities	owners
10. expertise	knowledge	experience	effort	interests

D. Use the words above to complete the following sentences.

1. There are many _____ that manufacture computers.

2. The _____ family was in need of food and clothing.

3. Through great effort he was able to _____ all hardships.

4. The town was _____ by the hurricane.

5. The carpenter used his _____ to build a cabinet.

6. The project completed with success because of their _____ .

7. Because the water was unclean, those who drank it became _____ .

8. She felt it was her _____ to go out and help the poor.

Basic Rules of Capitalization

Capitalize the following:

- abbreviations: A.D., B.C.
- main words in titles
- organizations and institutions
- days, months, holidays
- languages, races, nationalities, religions

- first words and I
- geographical names
- book titles, works of art
- historical names
- personal titles, proper nouns, and adjectives

E.   **Based on the rules above, cross out ✗ the wrongly-used small letters and replace them with capital letters.**

The number of capital letters required for each sentence is indicated in the ● .

1.   mr. johnson worked with uncle bob at the acme leather company.   **7**

2.   she read the bible on sunday and went to st. joseph's church.   **6**

3.   the book "cat in the hat" was written by dr. seuss.   **5**

4.   mike myers starred in the film "wayne's world".   **4**

5.   samuel de champlain established a settlement at quebec city in 1608.   **4**

6.   professor smith taught english at the university of toronto.   **5**

7.   the mona lisa, arguably the world's most famous painting, is on display in the louvre in paris.   **6**

8.   her birthday, january 2nd, is the day after new year's day.   **5**

9 The Blackout

On August 14, 2003 at 4:11 pm ET, lights went out across the north east United States and much of Ontario. Over 50 million people were in total darkness. The cause of the blackout was traced to the failure of an electrical plant in Ohio, which caused a domino effect knocking out power at plants across Ontario and the north east states. It was the largest electrical failure in history causing a memorable blackout that tested the resourcefulness of citizens and governments alike.

People in large urban areas were treated to a most unusual experience. There was no television or radio. Information was received only by battery-operated radios. Traffic lights were out causing chaos on busy city streets. Citizens took it upon themselves to man intersections acting as traffic police. People on their way home from work were stranded in subway tunnels. Streetcars were stalled in the middle of their routes. Refrigerators were no longer functional and food was going bad. People rushed to stores to stock up on canned and packaged goods only to find shops closed. Hospitals ran on auxiliary power and surgical operations were cancelled. Gas pumps were shut down so fuel was scarce. Candles flickered in homes for light, much like pioneer days.

The day after the blackout many people walked to work. Elevators were down so workers climbed flights of stairs to get to their offices only to find lights out and computers shut down. Life as we know it changed dramatically. Police and politicians, however, were amazed at the goodwill that spread throughout the cities.

For some the experience was an intolerable inconvenience, for others it was an exciting time. For many it was a time to look up to the night sky and, because of the total darkness, enjoy the splendour of the stars.

Cause and Effect

A cause is the reason for something or the reason an event occurs.
An effect is the end result of a cause.

A. **Give either the cause or the effect below. Feel free to give additional details beyond just the facts.**

1. Cause: _____

    Effect: People walked to work the day after the blackout.

2. Cause: A failure of an electrical plant in Ohio.

    Effect: _____

3. Cause: There was insufficient and unsafe power source in hospitals.

    Effect: _____

4. Cause: _____

    Effect: Workers climbed stairs.

5. Cause: _____

    Effect: The stars in the sky were unusually bright.

6. Cause: Food was going bad in refrigerators.

    Effect: _____

7. Cause: There was no television or electrical radio transmission of information.

    Effect: _____

8. Cause: _____

    Effect: Citizens took it upon themselves to conduct traffic at intersections.

9. Cause: Subway trains stopped suddenly.

    Effect: _____

Comma Use

A comma is used to:

- separate items in a series
- separate introductory words, phrases, or clauses
- set off persons being addressed
- separate the explanatory words of a direct quotation

- separate two adjectives in place of "and"
- with interruptive statements
- set off appositives
- separate the day, month, and year.

B.   Add the necessary commas to the following passage.

The New Student

Aisha Williams

On Monday September 9 a new student was admitted to our class. Our teacher Mr. Peters asked for the attention of the class. "Class" he said "I would like to introduce Aisha Williams a new student to our school." Instantly everyone turned and looked at the timid frightened girl by the door. Being a new student anyone would admit is not easy. After she was introduced she sat in her seat near the back of the room. Suddenly the recess bell rang and everyone got up to get their coats. At recess students have the following choices: play in the yard go to the library help teachers in the younger grades or answer phones in the office. A few of the students went up to Aisha introduced themselves and invited her to play in the yard. As expected she was shy at first but after a few minutes a big smile came to her face. Unfortunately just as she was getting comfortable playing with her new friends the bell rang again.

C. **Enhance the following passage with words from the word bank that create vivid and lively descriptions.**

Mark, the 1. _____ player on the team, was chosen to take the

2. _____ penalty shot that would 3. _____ the outcome of

the 4. _____ game. He 5. _____ at centre ice, and then

began his 6. _____ to the puck. The crowd was 7. _____ ,

8. _____ as he 9. _____ in long, slow strides towards the puck

ahead. The 10. _____ goalie waited in 11. _____ .

The crowd was dead 12. _____ . As he got close to the goal,

he 13. _____ and let fly a 14. _____ shot. The goalie

15. _____ across the net with his glove 16. _____ . With

17. _____ speed the puck 18. _____ off the goal post,

19. _____ off the goalie's pad, and 20. _____ into the net. The

red light 21. _____ and the crowd 22. _____ .

ricocheted	silent	critical	flickered
extended	nervous	determine	awestruck
championship	wound up	circled	
most talented	bounced	dove	
stunned	blistering	approach	roared
trickled	swayed	anticipation	lightning

89

10

When the British *Pop Idol* show was aired two years ago, no one could have imagined that this type of contest would spread around the globe. Countries throughout Europe, the Arab world, and North America each held their own "idol" contests. In Canada the *Canadian Idol* final show was the most watched event in Canadian television history.

In December, 2003 the eleven idols from around the world were flown to London, England to prepare for the ultimate contest – *World Idol*. Each contestant automatically received 12 points from his or her home country. Then, each country submitted votes for the other contestants: 10 points for first place, 9 for second, down to 1 point for 10th place. Most countries aired their preliminary shows on Christmas Day. The following week, the final contest was held and the voting results were kept secret until New Year's Day, 2004 when the gala event took place. Over 100 million people around the world tuned in, making *World Idol* the most watched television show of all time.

Of the 11 contestants, Kelly Clarkson of the US, a Grammy Award nominee, was the favourite to win. Ryan Malcolm, who beat out 16,000 other Canadian contestants, represented Canada with a brilliant performance. Exceptional performances from Australia's Guy Sebastian and Britain's Will Young made them strong contenders too. The most interesting performance came from Diana Karazon from the Arab nations – she sang a love song, "Ensami Ma Binsak", in her native language. The judges couldn't understand the song but praised her for choosing to sing in her own language.

When the excitement and anticipation ended and the votes were counted, the first *World Idol* was crowned. Kurt Nilsen of Norway, not considered to have had a chance of winning, was the unanimous choice of voters worldwide and named the first *World Idol*.

A. Refer to the passage. Write A, B, and C to indicate the order of events in each group.

1. [ ] The *Canadian Idol* contest was aired on television.

   [ ] The *World Idol* contest was aired on television.

   [ ] The British *Pop Idol* contest was aired on television.

2. [ ] Eleven idols were brought to London England.

   [ ] The eleven idols prepared for the ultimate contest.

   [ ] Eleven idols worldwide won contests.

3. [ ] The *World Idol* winner was announced.

   [ ] The final contest was held.

   [ ] Countries submitted their votes.

B. Test your recall. Match the World Idol events.

1. _____ nominated for the Grammy Award

2. _____ represented Great Britain

3. _____ title of an Arabic song

4. _____ number of Canadian contestants

5. _____ points awarded for 1st place

6. _____ on television in 2001

7. _____ points given by native country

8. _____ *World Idol* television viewers worldwide

9. _____ unanimous choice for *World Idol*

10. _____ represented Canada

A. Kurt Nilsen

B. 10 points

C. Ryan Malcolm

D. Will Young

E. over 100 million

F. 12 points

G. Kelly Clarkson

H. Ensami Ma Binsak

I. 16,000

J. British *Pop Idol*

Colons and Semicolons

Use a **colon**:

- to introduce items in a series
  Example: She needed the following items: milk, bread, butter, and tea.
- in a formal letter salutation
  Example: Dear Ms. Smith:
- before a statement that finishes the idea of a previous statement
  Example: He has one goal: to be the best.

Use a **semicolon**:

- to separate two short independent clauses (sentences) that are closely related in topic
  Example: She liked to sing; he liked to dance.

C. **In the following passage, insert colons or semicolons as needed.**

The Spelling Contest – **An Old Tradition**

Once a month, usually on a Friday, the teacher held a spelling contest. Many of the words were difficult to spell (   ) some impossible. The following examples are typically difficult words (   ) pneumonia, tonsillitis, recommendation, and magnificence. The teacher would read out the words (   ) the students would anxiously await their turn. A student would get two tries at a correct spelling (   ) a wrong answer meant you had to be seated. It was exciting (   ) however, it was also nerve-racking. When it came down to the final word, there was silence (   ) no one moved. Even if you were no longer in the contest, it was still exciting (   ) we would watch the final two contestants battle it out. Often a different person would win (   ) this is what made it fun. The teacher had one purpose in this contest (   ) students learning new words. The students had their own purpose (   ) winning the contest.

p-n-e-u-m-o-n-i-a

?

Simile, Personification, and Alliteration

A **simile** is a descriptive comparison between two things using "like" or "as".
Example: She was light <u>as a feather</u>.

Personification is the giving of human qualities to animals, inanimate objects, or ideas.
Example: The flowers danced in the breeze.

When two or more words are placed together with the same first letter, it is called an **alliteration**.
Example: **s**lippery **s**lope or **s**unsets, **s**ailboats and **s**ea breezes

D. In the following passage, add similes to make it more descriptive. Add an alliteration in the blank with a letter.

The Winter Storm

The 1. w _____ wind howled like 2. _____ through the bare trees that swayed like 3. _____ . The wind, as cold as 4. _____ burned their faces like a 5. _____ . As quick as 6. _____ , the children rushed home to the welcoming 7. w _____ of the fire. Once there, like 8. _____ they huddled together before the 9. f _____ flames placing their 10. f _____ fingers close to the fire. Mother brought steaming hot chocolate that tasted like 11. _____ . Soon they were as warm as 12. _____ .

Challenge

Create personification by adding human-like action words.

Example: The sun <u>kissed</u> the dew drops away.

1. The sputtering engine _____ slowly in the middle of the road.

2. The noisy gulls _____ at the picnickers.

3. The blazing sun _____ upon the sunbathers.

4. The wind _____ a warning of the storm to come.

A. Underline the adjectives and place parentheses ( ) around the adverbs in the following passage.

The Skating Party

Jenny and Samantha who were best friends decided to organize a skating party at the local arena. They intended to rent the arena and wisely charge everyone a small admission fee. Everyone enthusiastically responded immediately. Initially they thought that they would have great difficulty selling the necessary one hundred tickets but it was surprisingly easy. The first thing they did was sell tickets to their classmates and cleverly suggest that they all bring a neighbourhood friend or a favourite relative. Next, they posted an attractive sign outside the gymnasium. Soon half the tickets were sold. On the final day before the event, the last ticket was finally sold. The party was exciting. The popular music played loudly over the arena speakers and everyone had a wonderful time. Jenny and Samantha proudly declared that this would be an annual event.

B. Match each of the following words with its synonym.

1. catastrophe _____		A	plan
2. statistics _____		B	study
3. research _____		C	detailed
4. strategy _____		D	mathematical data
5. extensive _____		E	devastation

C. Put "F" for sentence fragments and "C" for complete sentences.

1. While shopping for sports equipment. _____

2. After school, they went tobogganing. _____

3. Although it was raining very hard. _____

4. Even if the team wins every remaining game. _____

5. Aside from going to the cottage, they will be home all summer. _____

6. Please wait for me. _____

7. As a matter of fact. _____

8. Having been to Winnipeg several times before. _____

D. Underline the adjective phrases and place parentheses ( ) around the adverb phrases in the following passage.

City Life, Country Life

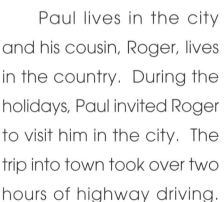

Paul lives in the city and his cousin, Roger, lives in the country. During the holidays, Paul invited Roger to visit him in the city. The trip into town took over two hours of highway driving. Roger, a boy from a farm, was amazed at the size of the tall buildings in the downtown core. He was used to open fields of corn, trails for horseback riding, and skies filled with stars at night. After his visit, he suggested to Paul that in the summer he come to the farm and enjoy two weeks of a complete lifestyle change.

E.   Cross out ✗ the small letters and replace them with capital letters where necessary.

if you live in toronto and you watch nhl hockey, chances are you are a maple leafs fan. you may even be lucky enough to get tickets to the air canada centre to watch a game. every saturday night, thousands of fans make their way to lakeshore boulevard to see their beloved leafs.

F.   Circle the best synonym for each of the following words in "Stephanie Dotto – Making a Difference".

1.	impoverished	improved	poor	destitute
2.	devastated	ruined	designed	surprised
3.	dedication	duty	endurance	denounce
4.	corporations	professionals	charities	companies
5.	images	formations	pictures	vision
6.	fate	failure	direction	destiny

G.   Select the proper verb for each sentence below. Write it in the blank.

1.   _____ take / bring the groceries into the house.

2.   _____ can / may he manage to lift the heavy boxes?

3.   He will _____ rise / raise his voice above the noise.

4.   She will _____ lie / lay the tablecloth on the dining room table.

5.   They _____ let / leave the dog go out every morning.

H. **Select the correct word for each sentence below. Write it in the blank.**

1. She will _____ accept / except the award at the ceremony.

2. There were _____ less / fewer people in attendance.

3. They shared the pizza _____ between / among the four of them.

4. She walked _____ into / in the room.

5. Please _____ bring / take this book to Cindy for me.

I. **Determine whether the underlined verbals are gerunds or participles. Write "G" for gerund or "P" for participle after each sentence.**

1. Snowboarding is his favourite winter pastime. _____

2. The falling snow soon covered the parked cars. _____

3. His running shoes were worn out. _____

4. The playing field was located beside the school. _____

5. The family enjoyed playing cards together. _____

6. He brought a pack of playing cards to the cottage. _____

J. **Underline the independent clauses and place parentheses around the dependent clauses in the following sentences.**

1. Before the guests arrived, they set the table.

2. They bought a new car because they were making a long trip.

3. If you don't dress warmly in this weather, you will freeze.

4. Whenever they exercise vigorously, they work up a sweat.

5. The students were relieved after they had written the test.

K. **Identify each sentence as compound "C" or compound-complex "CC".**

1. They tried to rehearse for the play but not everyone attended. _____

2. Because it was the third period, the hockey team pulled their goalie and tried to score a quick goal. _____

3. She painted a beautiful picture and she gave it to her mother. _____

4. Because they were in charge of raising money, they organized a bake sale but they had difficulty selling their goods. _____

5. Despite our best effort, our team lost the game in the end. _____

L. **Select the correct verb form for each sentence below. Write it in the blank.**

1. The number of runners in the race _____ is / are lower this year.

2. The computer programs _____ was / were educational.

3. Kara and Lauren _____ walk / walks home from school.

4. Paul and his friends _____ play / plays road hockey.

5. His mittens and jacket _____ was / were left on the bus.

M. **Select the correct homonym for each sentence below. Write it in the blank.**

1. The _____ border / boarder patrol checked passports.

2. They will _____ paws / pause to get a drink.

3. It was a _____ feet / feat of great courage.

4. She wore a _____ suede / swayed jacket.

5. The store sold a variety of _____ tease / teas .

N. State whether the italicized words are examples of simile, personification, or alliteration. Circle the correct description.

1. She ran *like the wind* and won the race.

       simile   personification   alliteration

2. *Time flies* when you are having fun.

       simile   personification   alliteration

3. *The sun smiled* on the flowers.

       simile   personification   alliteration

4. *The mountains huddled* together.

       simile   personification   alliteration

5. *The soaring seagulls* rose above the cliffs.

       simile   personification   alliteration

6. The moon *was like a ship* on a sea of clouds.

       simile   personification   alliteration

O. In the following sentences, add commas, colons, and semicolons where needed.

1. Before they bought their skis they compared prices.

2. She collected the following items antique dolls stamps and clocks.

3. The school is concerned with one thing the success of all students.

4. She was a volleyball player her brother preferred to play hockey.

5. Students should be hardworking not lazy.

6. The final game they all agreed was the best game of the season.

7. Paul his best friend lived next door.

Science

1

We classify the organisms that make up the living world so that we can understand and learn about them better. This classification is based on the body structure of the organism. The animal kingdom has many different types of organisms.

Invertebrates

dog   snail   turtle
jellyfish   hawk
octopus   snake
human being   shark
earthworm   centipede
grasshopper

Classify the twelve animals in the picture by placing them properly in the chart.

Animals without backbones are called **invertebrates**. Animals with backbones are called **vertebrates**.

①

Invertebrate	Vertebrate

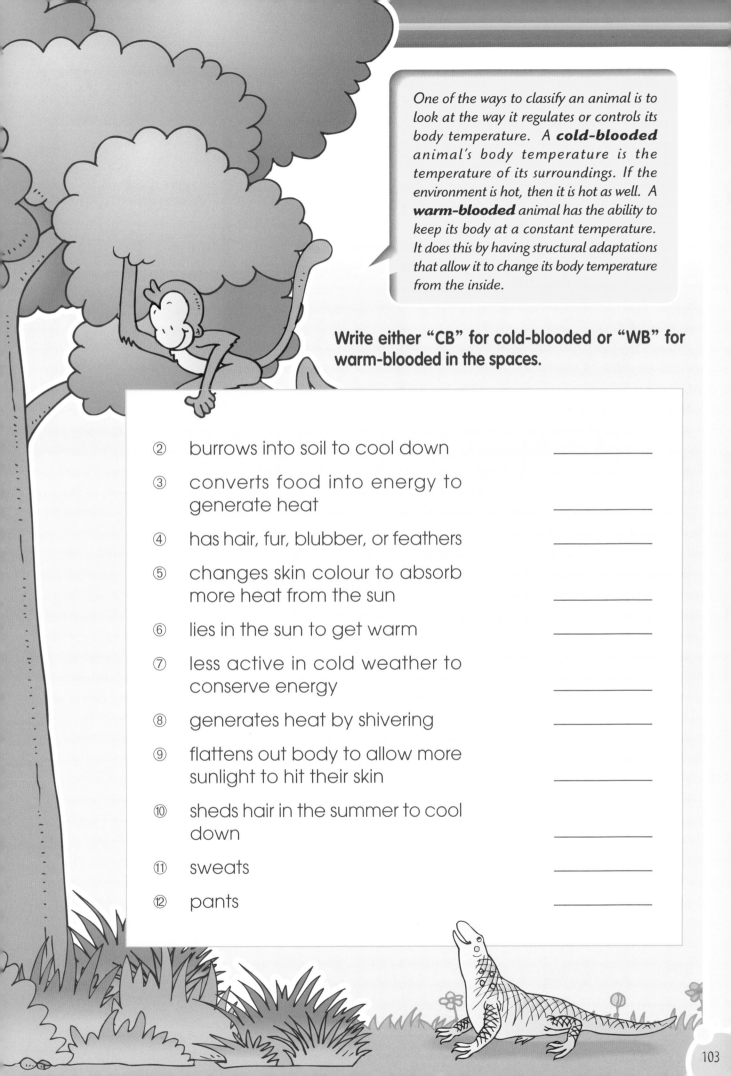

One of the ways to classify an animal is to look at the way it regulates or controls its body temperature. A **cold-blooded** animal's body temperature is the temperature of its surroundings. If the environment is hot, then it is hot as well. A **warm-blooded** animal has the ability to keep its body at a constant temperature. It does this by having structural adaptations that allow it to change its body temperature from the inside.

Write either "CB" for cold-blooded or "WB" for warm-blooded in the spaces.

② burrows into soil to cool down _____

③ converts food into energy to generate heat _____

④ has hair, fur, blubber, or feathers _____

⑤ changes skin colour to absorb more heat from the sun _____

⑥ lies in the sun to get warm _____

⑦ less active in cold weather to conserve energy _____

⑧ generates heat by shivering _____

⑨ flattens out body to allow more sunlight to hit their skin _____

⑩ sheds hair in the summer to cool down _____

⑪ sweats _____

⑫ pants _____

Help Mary complete her project on invertebrates. Label the pictures and match them with the notes. Write the letters.

⑬

I'm trying to classify the invertebrates, based on body structure.

mollusks   arthropods   sea anemones
sand dollars   sponges   worms

⑭ tube-shaped body; different cells do different jobs; filter feeders; water flows through bodies; certain cells filter out food

⑮ simple bag within a bag body design; two cell layers; stinging cells on tentacles; includes hydra and jellyfish

⑯ flat, round, and segmented; some are parasitic (they live inside other animals); the earthworm is highly developed in its organ systems

⑰ tough, jointed exoskeleton; segmented body; the most successful animal on the planet; found anywhere there's land; includes insects

⑱ have a one- or two-part shell; some have a muscular foot that they use with slime to move upon; snails, clams, and octopuses

⑲ ocean dwellers; have rays or arms; a water-filled canal system and tube feet that allow for movement; starfish, seastars

Answer the questions with the given words.

> three   cockroach   sense organs   legs
> arthropod   insects   thorax   dragonfly   exoskeleton

⑳ To what phylum do insects belong? _____

㉑ Which are the most diverse animals on the planet? _____

㉒ What houses the many organs of an insect? _____

㉓ What do insects have so that they can detect light, sound, temperature, and odour? _____

㉔ How many segments is an insect's body divided into? _____

㉕ Which section of an insect bears the legs and wings? _____

㉖ Insects have three pairs of these. What are they? _____

㉗ What kind of insect can fly up to speeds of 55 km/h? _____

㉘ What kind of insect can "live" for about a week with its head cut off? _____

In each group of invertebrates below, which one is an insect? Circle it.

㉙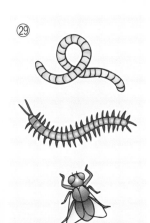

㉚

㉛

㉜

105

2 Scientists have put organisms into groups based on their body structure. Animals with backbones are called **vertebrates**. They have an internal skeleton made of bones and both left and right parts of the body are the same.

Diverse Vertebrates

Match each class of vertebrates with the correct description. Then give examples to each class. Write the letters.

① _____

- soft, moist, naked skin
- cold-blooded
- eggs laid by most

- e.g. _____

② _____

- live birth; young nursed by mother
- warm-blooded
- hair or fur

- e.g. _____

③ _____

- overlapping dry scales
- cold-blooded
- eggs laid by most

- e.g. _____

④ _____

- wet scales and mucus
- cold-blooded
- lay eggs

- e.g. _____

⑤ _____

- feathers
- warm-blooded
- lay eggs

- e.g. _____

The Five Classes of Vertebrates

Amphibian **Fish** **Reptile**

Bird **Mammal**

- **A** Ostrich
- **B** Salamander
- **C** Bullfrog
- **D** Rattlesnake
- **E** Hummingbird
- **F** Human being
- **G** Cod
- **H** Whale
- **I** Shark
- **J** Crocodile

The skin is a very important organ. It protects the animal's organs from the environment. It can also camouflage the animal, helping it to survive among predators and prey.

Look at the pattern of each of the following body coverings. Then name it using the given word.

Cheetah Fish
Elephant Snake
Duck Frog

⑥

A _____ B _____

C _____ D _____

E _____ F _____

The diversity of the lives of vertebrates has led to many odd ways of getting from one place to another.

In the following chart, write the name of a vertebrate that normally spends a good portion of its life living in that "space". Name the body part(s) that helps it move about.

⑦

Mode \ Class	Fish	Amphibian	Reptile	Bird	Mammal
On Land					
In Water	Salmon (fins and tail)				
In Air					

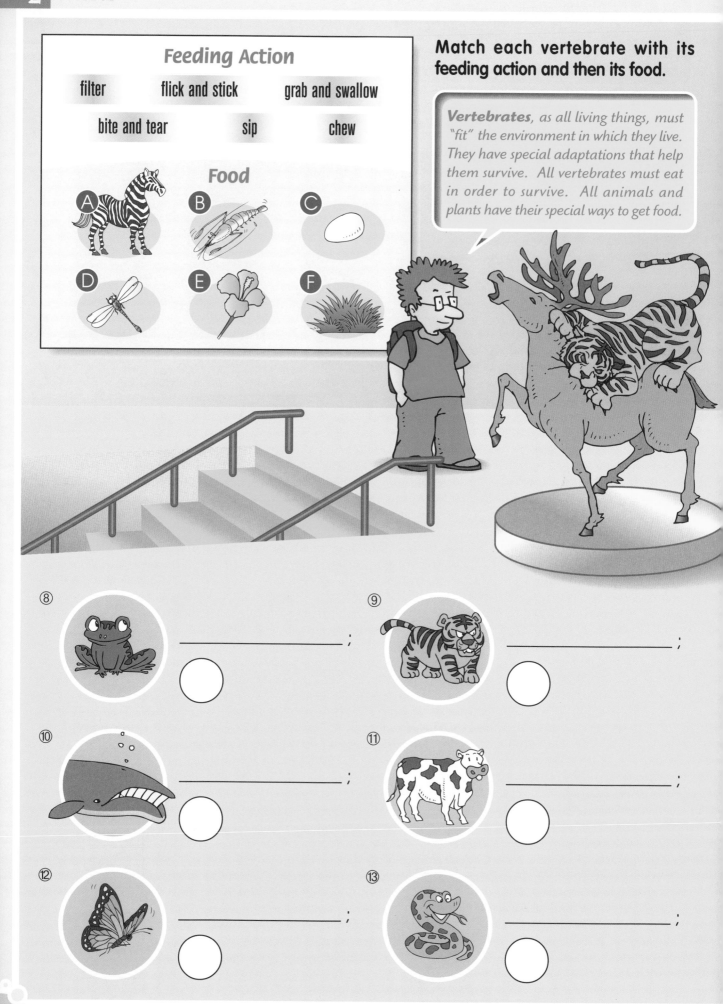

Feeding Action

filter   flick and stick   grab and swallow

bite and tear   sip   chew

Food

A

B

C

D

E

F

Match each vertebrate with its feeding action and then its food.

Vertebrates, as all living things, must "fit" the environment in which they live. They have special adaptations that help them survive. All vertebrates must eat in order to survive. All animals and plants have their special ways to get food.

⑧ _____ ;

⑨ _____ ;

⑩ _____ ;

⑪ _____ ;

⑫ _____ ;

⑬ _____ ;

Identify each of the creatures being talked about. Then state whether or not you think the parents would stay around to raise the offspring.

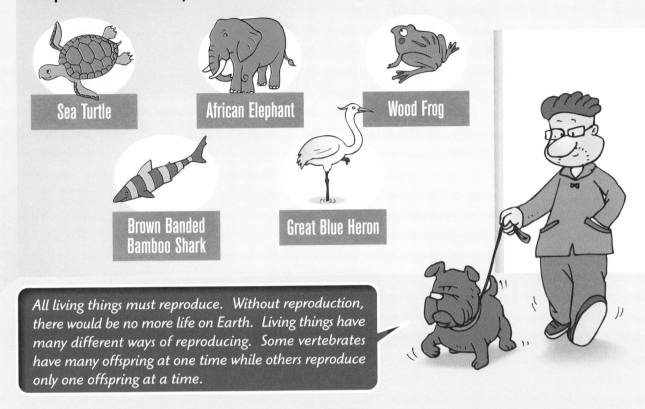

Sea Turtle

African Elephant

Wood Frog

Brown Banded Bamboo Shark

Great Blue Heron

All living things must reproduce. Without reproduction, there would be no more life on Earth. Living things have many different ways of reproducing. Some vertebrates have many offspring at one time while others reproduce only one offspring at a time.

⑭ They have been known to give birth to as many as 50 live babies at a time. The pups look like smaller versions of their parents, and can swim and hunt on their own.

_____

⑮ Some lay up to 800 eggs in a jelly mass... hatch in 15 – 20 days.

_____

⑯ A female will go up on the beach and lay up to 150 eggs in the sand. When they hatch, it's a wild scramble to the ocean. Watch out for the gulls.

_____

⑰ A typical female will give birth every four to six years. The newborn weighs 100 kg and stands about a metre in height.

_____

⑱ Three to seven eggs are laid in the spring.

_____

3  Air: All about It

There's evidence of air in this picture! Can you find nine things that indicate air is there? List them below.

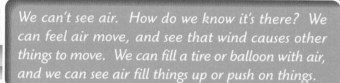

We can't see air. How do we know it's there? We can feel air move, and see that wind causes other things to move. We can fill a tire or balloon with air, and we can see air fill things up or push on things.

① **Evidence of air:**

_____ _____ _____

_____ _____ _____

_____ _____ _____

Follow the steps to do the experiment. Then answer the questions.

Step 1

Stretch a balloon over an open, empty water bottle.

Step 2

Place the bottle in a sink of very warm water.

expand

warm water

Step 3

Empty the warm water and fill the sink with ice water.

compress

ice water

②   When the bottle is placed in the sink with warm water, what happens?

_____

③   When the bottle is placed in the sink with ice water, what happens?

_____

> *Air expands when heated because the molecules are further apart. This also has the effect of making warm air lighter.*

Circle the correct endings to complete the sentences.

④   Warm air meets cooler air. The warm air expands and

   rises   falls .

⑤   A mobile hung from a ceiling is gently moving. The heat

   radiator below it is   off   on .

⑥   The temperature in a house is normally cooler on the

   bottom   top   floor.

⑦   A bird gliding in the sky is riding on the rising   warm   cool   air.

Read the paragraph. Then write "compressed" or "insulating" to tell what kind of air each picture shows.

Two qualities of air enable us to use it as a useful tool. Air can be compressed, and air can act as an insulator. **Compressed air** is when more than the regular amount of air has been pushed into a container. More air in the same space exerts more pressure. Air acts as an **insulator** when it helps to conserve heat.

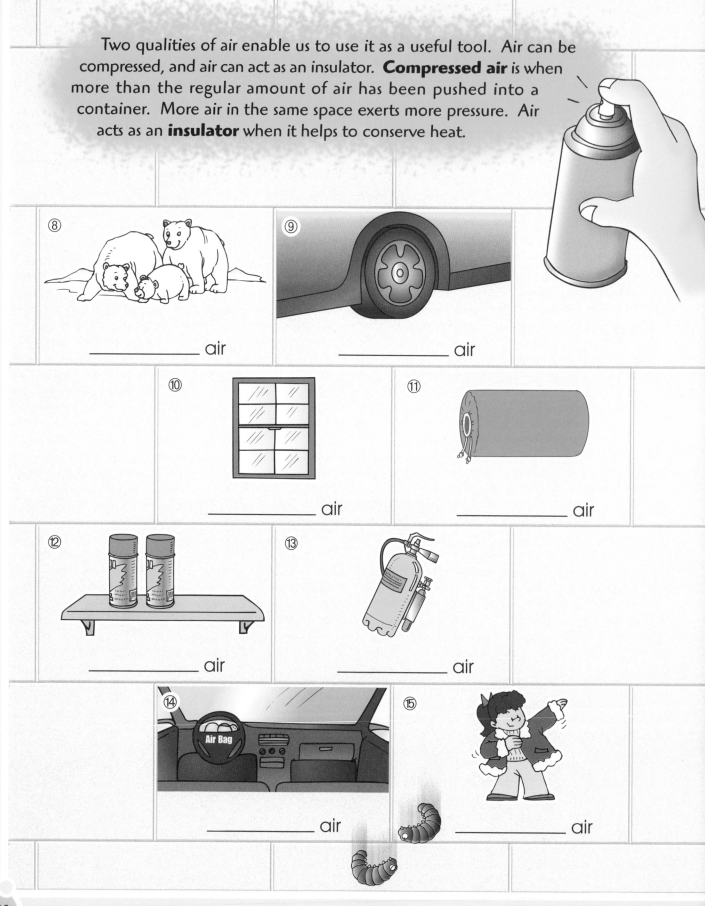

⑧ _____ air

⑨ _____ air

⑩ _____ air

⑪ _____ air

⑫ _____ air

⑬ _____ air

⑭ _____ air

⑮ _____ air

These facts about air demonstrate some of the properties of air. Match each fact with the property. Write the letter.

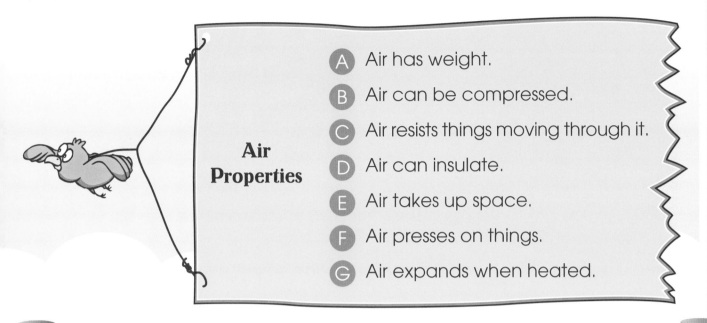

Air Properties

A Air has weight.

B Air can be compressed.

C Air resists things moving through it.

D Air can insulate.

E Air takes up space.

F Air presses on things.

G Air expands when heated.

Air Facts

⑯ A feather down coat traps air within it. It keeps the warmth in and the cold out. ◯

⑰ Air molecules move around and spread out when heated. ◯

⑱ An "empty" water bottle, when immersed in water upside down, will not fill with water because it is already full of air! ◯

⑲ A flat car tire is lighter than when it was full of air. ◯

⑳ A card, placed over the rim of a cup full of water, will hold the water in place while the cup is upside down. The only thing holding the card in place is the air underneath the card. ◯

㉑ A flat piece of paper falls slower to the ground than a crumpled piece of paper. ◯

㉒ Air expands to fill a container, but we may put still more air in it. ◯

4

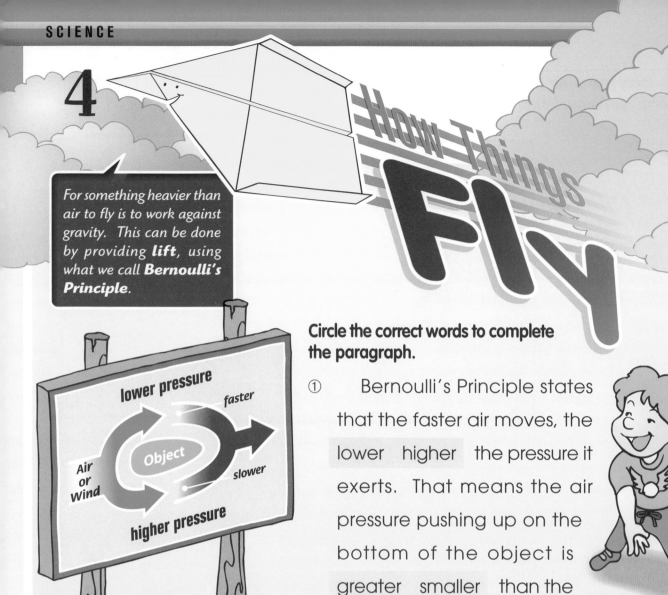

How Things FLY

For something heavier than air to fly is to work against gravity. This can be done by providing **lift**, using what we call **Bernoulli's Principle**.

lower pressure

faster

Object

Air or Wind

slower

higher pressure

Circle the correct words to complete the paragraph.

① Bernoulli's Principle states that the faster air moves, the lower higher the pressure it exerts. That means the air pressure pushing up on the bottom of the object is greater smaller than the pressure pushing down, so the object goes up.

What will happen in these instances of unbalanced air pressure? Draw arrows to show the movement of the object caused by the unbalanced air pressure.

② still air

still air

faster air

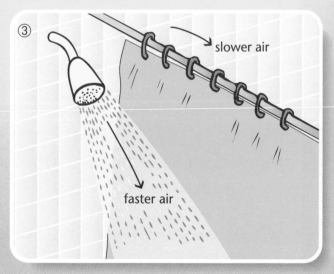

③ slower air

faster air

Match each flying machine or animal with its source of propulsion.

(A) moving air (B) rocket

(C) human muscle energy

(D) engine (E) propeller

(F) wing

Thrust is the force that propels something through the air.

④

⑤

⑥

⑦

⑧

⑨

The force opposing the thrust is called the **drag**. Drag is what must be overcome for something to move forward through air. Drag must be increased, though, to slow down or stop. An airplane flying at a steady speed has a balanced force of thrust and drag.

Draw an arrow to show the drag in each picture.

⑩

⑪

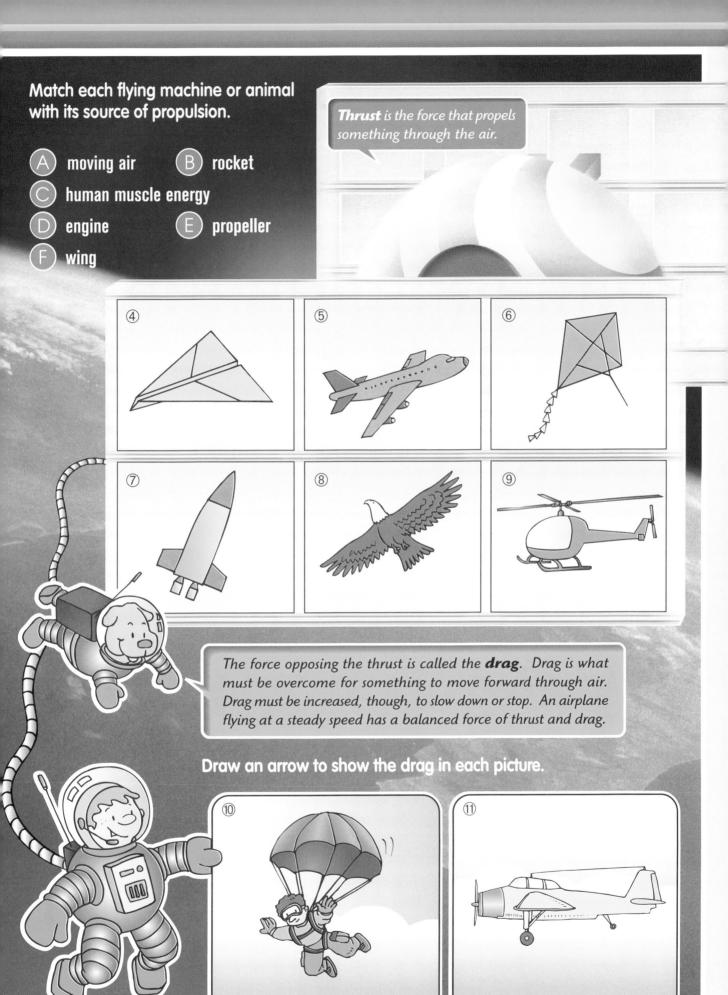

Hold a paper strip below your mouth and blow over the top of it. Can you see how the paper is pushed upwards? Answer the questions.

⑫ Where was the faster moving air?

Ⓐ above the paper   Ⓑ below the paper

⑬ Where was the high pressure air?

Ⓐ above the paper   Ⓑ below the paper

Check ✔ the pictures that are examples of airfoil providing lift.

Bernoulli's Principle helps explain how an airplane or a bird can gain **lift**, the force that acts against gravity. The shape of a wing is called an **airfoil**, and is the cause of the unbalanced air pressure above and below the wing. The air must move farther and faster over the top of the wing.

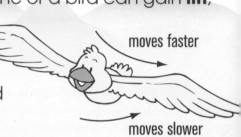

moves faster

moves slower

⑭
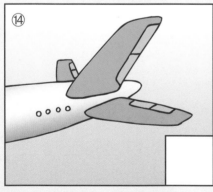

⑮

⑯

⑰
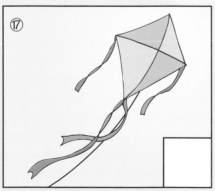

⑱

⑲

In each pair of objects below, one has a more streamlined form than the other. Circle it.

*When something is built to reduce drag, we say it is **streamlined**. Streamline helps objects reduce drag on the ground and in the water, as well as in the air.*

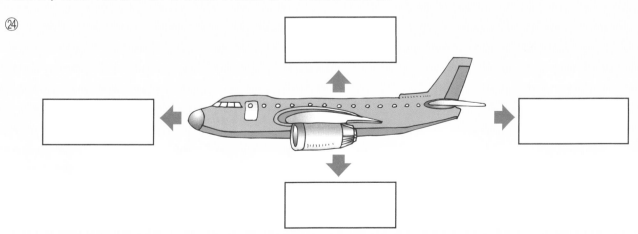

Read the paragraph and label the diagram with the bold words. Then answer the question.

Something flying at a steady speed has balanced forces of **thrust** and **drag**. If it is flying at a steady altitude, it has balanced forces of **gravity** and **lift**. Sometimes the forces are not balanced. For example, in order to go faster, the force of thrust must be increased.

㉔

㉕ Which two forces have to be increased in order for the airplane to ascend? _____ and _____

5

There are two types of electricity: static and current. **Static electricity** is what you feel when you touch a doorknob after shuffling across the carpet. When things are rubbed, they can become electrically charged. **Current electricity** is much more useful to us. It can be transformed into light, heat, and motion energy.

Electricity

Write "S" for static electricity or "C" for current electricity in this home.

Try This!

> A **conductor** is a substance that allows electric current to flow through it. We use these materials to build circuits. An **insulator** is a substance that electricity cannot flow through.

Materials

- a battery
- a screwdriver
- masking tape
- a bulb holder and a bulb
- 3 wires

Directions

1. Tape and connect the wires with the battery and the bulb holder as shown.

2. Place one bare wire at one end of an object and the second bare wire at the other end. If the bulbs lights up, it means that the object is a conductor; otherwise, it is an insulator.

Collect the things shown on the table. Then use the above experiment to test the things. List them in the correct columns.

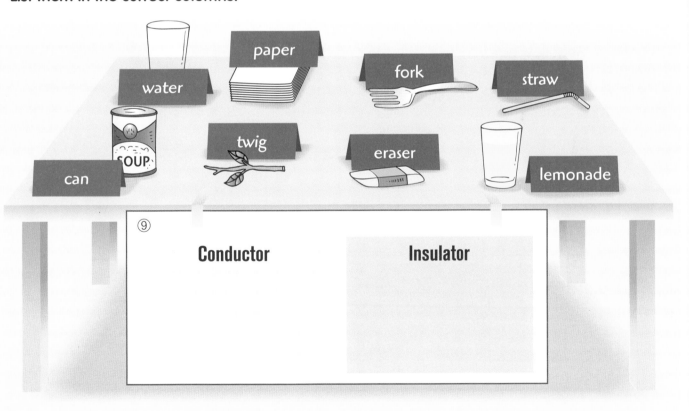

⑨

Conductor	Insulator

Using the information gathered from the chart above, write "conductor" or "insulator" to describe the following materials.

⑩ Water _____

⑪ Metal _____

⑫ Rubber _____

⑬ Wood _____

Label the symbols with the given words.

⑭
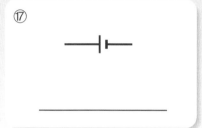

_____

⑮

_____

⑯
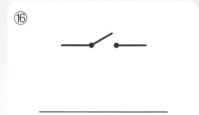

_____

⑰
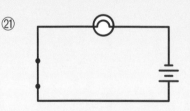

_____

cell   light bulb   switch   wire

Look at the following circuits. Circle the problem area if there is something preventing the flow of current. Write "CC" if it is a closed circuit.

⑱
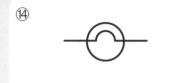

_____

⑲
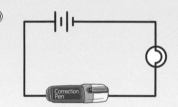

Correction Pen

_____

⑳
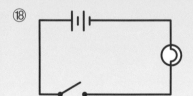

_____

㉑
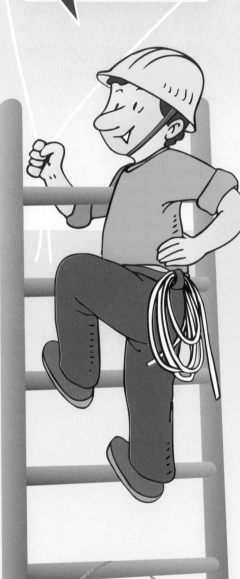

_____

㉒
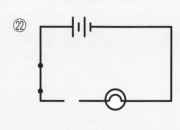

_____

㉓
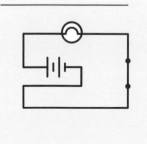

_____

In drawing circuits, different symbols are used for each component. Through these drawings, we all understand and "speak" the same language.

For an electric current to flow, it must have a continuous route to travel. It must go from the source, through the electrical device, and back to the source. That is called a **closed circuit**.

120

Fill in the blanks with the given words to complete what Edward says.

More than one electrical device can share the same power source. Sometimes the devices are connected along the same ㉔ _____ path, one after the other. This is a ㉕ _____ circuit. Most times, devices are connected in a ㉖ _____ circuit. For this, they individually have their own path from and back to the ㉗ _____ .

parallel
series
single
power source

Are the circuits parallel or in series ? List them in the correct boxes.

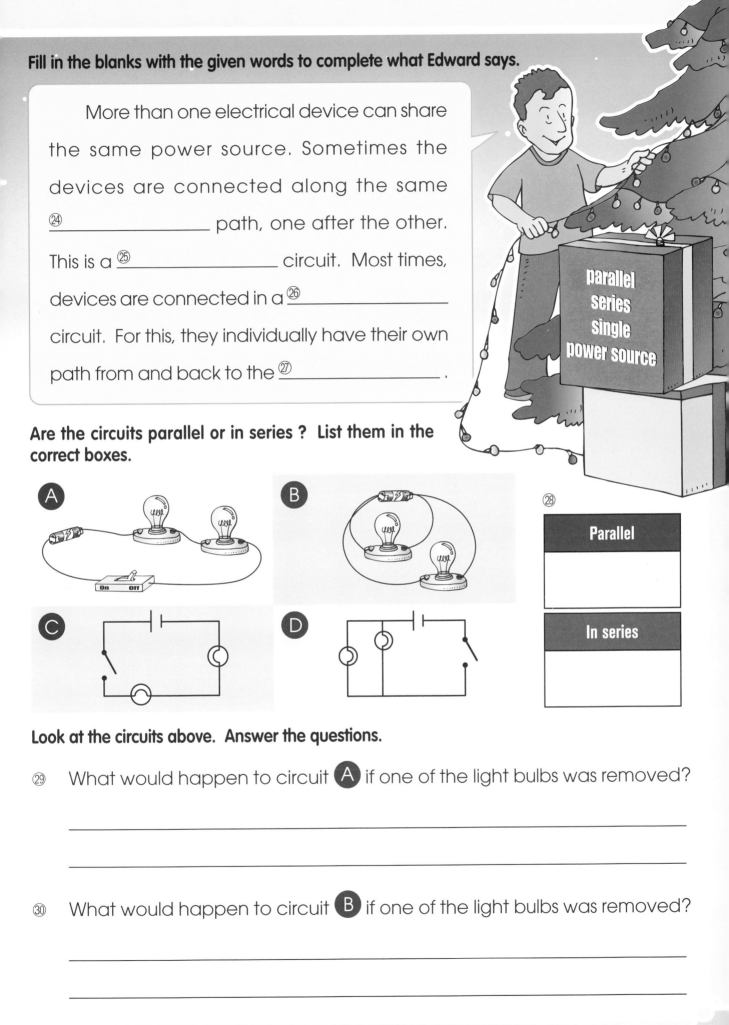

A

B

㉘

Parallel

C

D

In series

Look at the circuits above. Answer the questions.

㉙ What would happen to circuit **A** if one of the light bulbs was removed?

_____

_____

㉚ What would happen to circuit **B** if one of the light bulbs was removed?

_____

_____

6 More about Electricity

Read the paragraph. Then tell whether the sentences are true (T) or false (F).

More than 200 years ago in Italy, scientist **Luigi Galvani** accidentally touched two different metals together during a dead frog dissection. The frog's leg jerked. Galvani wondered if he'd discovered an electrical force in the frog's body. He didn't. But what he did discover was electricity that was very different from static electricity and lightning.

Allessandro Volta, around 1800, invented the first battery. Galvani's discovery helped him in his invention, which used two different metals and salty water, instead of frog fluids. Before the invention of battery, electric machines worked on static electricity, and only for very short periods.

*What led us to be using electricity the way we do today? Ancient peoples, it is believed, knew about current electricity. But that didn't lead them to use it. **Luigi Galvani** and **Allessandro Volta** are two people who experimented and learned a lot about electricity.*

① Volta did experiments on frogs. _____

② Galvani was using two different kinds of metals. _____

③ These discoveries took place around 200 years ago. _____

④ Galvani knew what he had discovered. _____

⑤ Electric machines once worked only with lightning. _____

⑥ Volta's invention was independent of other discoveries. _____

⑦ What Galvani discovered was different from static electricity and lightning. _____

*The electrical energy we use can come from **renewable** or **non-renewable** sources. The non-renewable sources are the ones that will sooner or later run out, but all sources have some disadvantages.*

Read the descriptions and match them with the sources. Then tell whether they are "renewable" or "non-renewable".

⑧ Heat energy and light energy from the sun is less polluting but expensive.

_____ ; _____

⑨ It is produced with the help of the mineral uranium; the waste this form of energy produces is long-lived and dangerous.

_____ ; _____

⑩ Windmills transform moving air to electricity. They are less polluting, but they are not without problems.

_____ ; _____

⑪ It takes millions of years in the making; this underground solid is a serious pollutant when burned for energy.

_____ ; _____

⑫ It is not polluting, but the negative impact dams have on the physical environment and nature is large.

_____ ; _____

⑬ Millions of years ago, it was dead plants and animals; now we find the liquid between layers of rocks underground.

_____ ; _____

Solar   Moving water   Nuclear   Coal   Wind   Oil

Match the modern activities that use electricity with similar activities before electricity was used. Write the letters.

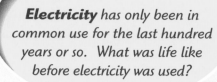
Electricity has only been in common use for the last hundred years or so. What was life like before electricity was used?

Modern

Before Electricity

⑭ electric washer and dryer ◯ Ⓐ wood stove

⑮ microwave oven ◯ Ⓑ gas lamp

⑯ people watching T.V. ◯ Ⓒ steam and coal fired train

⑰ light bulb ◯ Ⓓ people talking, playing games

⑱ computer ◯ Ⓔ wringer washer and clothesline

⑲ sewing machine ◯ Ⓕ thread and needle

⑳ electric train/subway ◯ Ⓖ manual typewriter, paper, and pen

List three other things you use today that are powered by electricity.

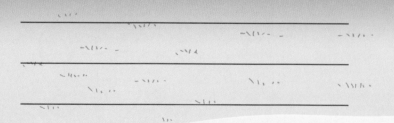

㉑ _____

_____

_____

What would have been used in their place in the times before electricity was in common use?

㉒ _____

_____

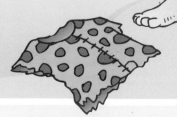

Find the electricity words in the puzzle. They may be backward, forward, and diagonal.

current   electric   battery
circuit   conductor
insulator   series   Galvani
renewable   Volta   parallel
non-renewable

23

C	C	A	M	A	R	U	H	I	A	G	T
I	O	T	D	F	K	T	N	D	A	W	T
R	N	L	G	J	N	S	O	L	E	M	C
C	D	O	A	T	U	B	V	L	J	M	I
U	U	V	E	L	B	A	W	E	N	E	R
I	C	W	A	R	N	T	S	L	M	W	T
T	T	T	F	I	N	Z	V	L	T	S	C
N	O	N	R	E	N	E	W	A	B	L	E
R	R	D	R	W	S	E	I	R	E	S	L
O	S	R	P	S	G	K	H	A	L	X	E
V	U	O	S	T	R	X	T	P	F	Y	A
C	B	A	T	T	E	R	Y	L	C	E	Q

Science
Fact

When you plug in, make sure your hands and the floor are dry.

Water is one of the best conductors of electricity. Your body is mostly water, and that makes you a good conductor, too.

7

Motion, or movement, happens when something changes position. But did you know things move in different ways, and there are "laws" that movement follows?

Motion

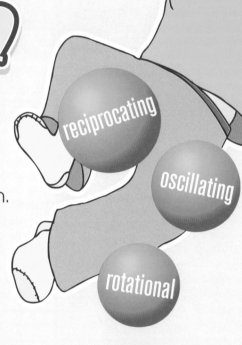

Fill in the blanks with the given words.

There are four ways to describe the way things move. ① _____ motion is one that moves in a straight line and in one direction. ② _____ motion is one that follows a circular path. A motion back and forth from a central point is ③ _____ motion. ④ _____ motion is a back-and-forth movement in a straight line.

reciprocating

oscillating

rotational

linear

Look at the motion path of each kind of motion. Then label each picture with "linear", "oscillating", "rotational", or "reciprocating".

⑤

_____ motion

⑥

_____ motion

How are these things move? Look at the highlighted parts. Draw the motion paths. Then put the movements in the correct boxes.

⑨

A

B

C

D

E

F

Motion	
⑩	
Linear	Oscillating
Rotational	Reciprocating

⑦

_____ motion

⑧

_____ motion

Do the people need to increase or reduce friction? Circle the correct words and check ✔ the correct methods.

⑪ I want to increase the speed of my car.

increase   **reduce**   friction

Ⓐ drive a streamlined racing car

Ⓑ drive a heavy racing car

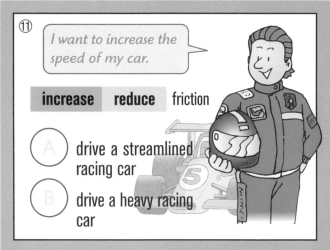

⑫ In a tug-of-war game, how can we beat our opponents?

increase   **reduce**   friction

Ⓐ wear shoes without treads

Ⓑ wear shoes with treads

⑬ I can hear the metal grinding!

increase   **reduce**   friction

Ⓐ add oil to the engine

Ⓑ dry the engine

⑭ How can I walk with higher stability on the balance beam?

increase   **reduce** friction

Ⓐ wear socks

Ⓑ walk barefoot

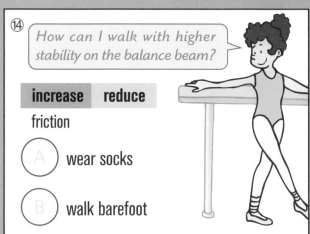

An object in motion will stay in motion until another force acts on it. The force that no moving object on Earth can avoid is friction. **Friction** is the force of two surfaces rubbing against each other. It is stronger with rough surfaces and weaker with smooth or wet surfaces.

Science Fact

What kind of motion does an ocean wave have? Rotational! Believe it or not, waves go down and up in a circular motion.

Read the clues and complete the crossword puzzle.

Across

A   a force that opposes motion

B   back-and-forth linear motion

C   causes all new motion

D   a change in position

Down

1   the motion of a wheel

2   the way a pendulum moves

3   straight-line motion

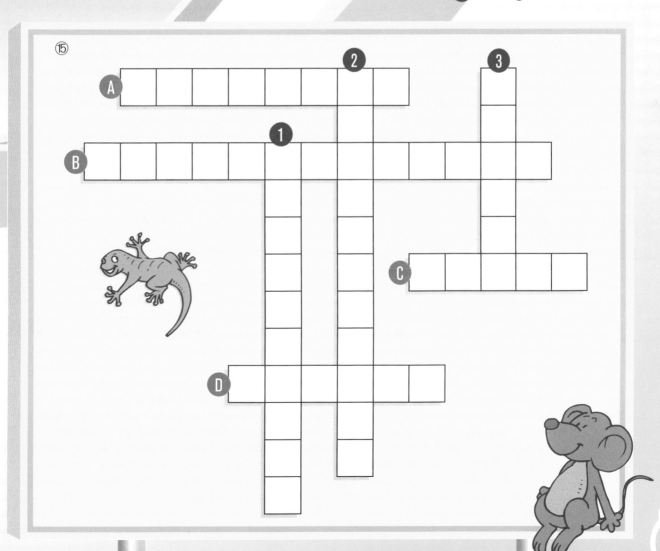

8 Motion and Machines

Find what simple machines they are. Write the letters.

A Inclined plane
B Wheel and axle
C Pulley
D Wedge
E Screw
F Lever

Machines make the job of moving things easier. All machines are made up of a simple machine or a combination of them.

Identify the simple machines. Write the letters. Then answer the question.

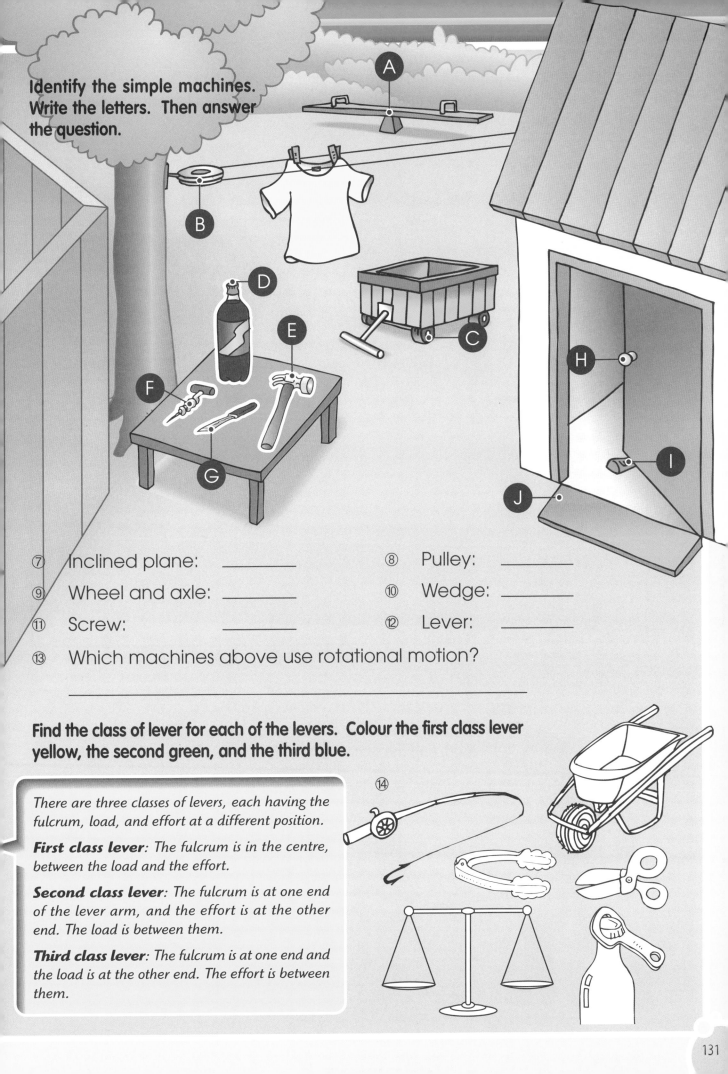

⑦ Inclined plane: _____

⑧ Pulley: _____

⑨ Wheel and axle: _____

⑩ Wedge: _____

⑪ Screw: _____

⑫ Lever: _____

⑬ Which machines above use rotational motion?

_____

Find the class of lever for each of the levers. Colour the first class lever yellow, the second green, and the third blue.

There are three classes of levers, each having the fulcrum, load, and effort at a different position.

First class lever: *The fulcrum is in the centre, between the load and the effort.*

Second class lever: *The fulcrum is at one end of the lever arm, and the effort is at the other end. The load is between them.*

Third class lever: *The fulcrum is at one end and the load is at the other end. The effort is between them.*

⑭

You have been given the job of lifting a huge pumpkin onto a wagon. Design a lever to help you. Don't forget to show the load (pumpkin) and effort force (you) in your drawing. Then answer the question.

⑮

lever arm	fulcrum	load	effort
——————	▲	➡	▪▪➡

⑯ What class of lever did you draw? _____

⑰ Gabriel's shovel is a lever, too. Where is the fulcrum, the load, and the effort? Label them. Then answer the question.

⑱ What class of lever is the shovel?

_____

Draw arrows to show the direction of motion for each lever in these linkage systems.

*A **linkage system** involves two or more levers working together. It can change the direction of a motion or make two mechanisms work together.*

⑲

⑳

㉑

Be an inventor! Move the marble from the table to the inside of the cup using two or more simple machines.

You may provide the initial effort required to put the marble into motion, in an up–down direction only. Draw your combination of simple machines.

40 cm

㉒

9 Earth and Our Solar System

Complete the sentences with the words on the asteroid.

year   orbit
day   axis
northern
southern

① The Earth is spinning on its _____ .

② The Earth's movement around the sun is called an _____ .

③ It's July. The _____ hemisphere is getting more direct sunlight. It's summer there now.

④ When the Earth is on the other side of the sun, it's summer in the _____ hemisphere.

⑤ It takes one _____ for the Earth to travel around the sun.

⑥ The Earth does a complete rotation, or spin, in one _____ .

Solve the riddle.

What lights our night sky yet emits no light?
What's always a sphere but seems different each night?
What spins round, yet shows only one side?
What causes, on Earth, the high and low tide?

⑦ [   ]

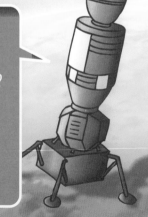

The moon goes through a change in appearance that we call **phases.** *Because the moon produces no light of its own, we can only see what is reflected off of it from the sun. Half of the moon is always lit up by the sun, but sometimes we see only a part of that. Half of the moon always faces us, but sometimes that includes an unlit part of the moon.*

Look at the pictures of the relative positions of the sun, Earth, and moon. Match the pictures. Write names in the boxes.

| Full moon | Old crescent | First quarter | New moon | Waning gibbous | New crescent | Waxing gibbous | Last quarter |

⑧

⑨

⑩

⑪

⑫

⑬

⑭

⑮

S – Sun   **E** – Earth   **M** – Moon

"**Waxing**" means growing.   "**Waning**" means shrinking.

"**Gibbous**" means swollen on one side or humpbacked.

Try This!   It's easy to memorize the order of the planets from the sun! Make up a sentence with each word beginning with the first letter of each of the planets. It may be serious or silly.

Mercury **V**enus **E**arth **M**ars **J**upiter **S**aturn **U**ranus **N**eptune **P**luto

⑯   M_____   V_____   E_____   M_____   J_____

      S_____   U_____   N_____   P_____

Solve the riddles with the help of the given words.

Earth   Venus   asteroid
moon   Jupiter   comet
Saturn   Pluto   Mars   Uranus
Mercury   Neptune

⑰   I am a natural satellite belonging to Earth. I have no water or air.   _____

⑱   Of all the gas planets, I'm known for my rings. The others also have some, but I have the most.   _____

⑲   I'm farthest from the sun, but I'm rocky, like the closest ones.   _____

⑳   I'm small and orbit the sun with many others like me.   _____

Science Fact

With the invention of the first telescope, about four hundred years ago, four satellites (moons) were discovered to be orbiting Jupiter. Today's technology has brought that count to 61 and counting. Jovian moons have been discovered as recently as 2003!

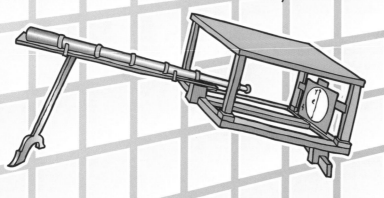

IO
EUROPA
GANYMEDE
CALLISTO
METIS
ADRASTEA
AMALTHEA
THEBE
LEDA
LYSITHEA
ELARA
ANANKE
CARME
PASIPHAE
SINOPE
HIMALIA

㉑ I am the largest planet, made mostly of hydrogen and helium. Another clue is my many moons.   _____

㉒ I am a rocky inner planet. I appear reddish from Earth because of the iron oxide in my soil.   _____

㉓ Unlike most of the others, I rotate east to west. I'm the hottest, and often mistaken for a bright white star.   _____

㉔ When you see me, I'm spectacular, but I'm just a dirty ball of ice.   _____

㉕ Third planet from the sun, my surface is mostly water.   _____

㉖ In orbit between Saturn and Neptune, my axis is such that I appear to be lying down.   _____

㉗ I'm the closest planet to the sun. I'm much smaller than Earth and have no moons.   _____

㉘ The last of the gas giants, I was named for the God of the Sea.   _____

Find the names from this list of some of the moons so far discovered.

㉙

L	M	T	A	O	R	G	U	E	C	O	S	V
A	E	U	R	O	P	A	I	C	A	R	M	E
E	T	R	A	L	E	N	B	S	O	T	B	N
T	I	A	L	P	L	Y	S	I	T	H	E	A
S	S	I	E	N	U	M	F	N	S	E	Q	A
A	M	A	L	T	H	E	A	O	I	B	S	N
R	Q	S	K	O	N	D	E	P	L	E	D	A
D	T	E	N	N	O	E	I	E	L	V	R	N
A	T	B	H	I	M	A	L	I	A	M	F	K
R	P	A	S	I	P	H	A	E	C	V	O	E

10 The  Night Sky

Northern lights Constellation
Meteoroids Satellite
Planet Milky Way
Stars Comet Moon

A

Some of the objects in the night sky can be seen every night; others, like comets, happen rarely.

Match the objects and names with the descriptions. Write the names in the boxes and the letters in the circles.

①

Looking like milk spilled across the night sky, this is the galaxy we are a part of.

②

It is a group of stars that, as seen from Earth, seems to form a picture.

③

They are spheres of hot gas. Except for one, they are so far away from us it is hard to comprehend.

④

It may look like a star in the sky, but this sunlight reflector doesn't twinkle, unless it is near the horizon.

⑤

This is, so far, the only celestial body humankind have stepped foot on.

⑥

Put in orbit by human beings as a technological tool, it can be seen slowly moving across the sky when it reflects the sunlight.

⑦

Like a colourful light show, they are caused by particles from the sun mixing with gases in Earth's upper atmosphere.

⑧

It is believed to be a mixture of ice, rock, and gas from a distance outside the solar system. It orbits the sun and has a distinct tail.

⑨

They are sometimes called "shooting stars" because that's what these broken bits of rock look like when they enter Earth's atmosphere.

Look at the shape of the constellations below. Find them on the star map and write the names.

Orion

Cygnus

Pegasus

Cassiopeia

Draco

Leo

Groups of stars as seen from Earth form patterns called **constellations**. The sky was mapped thousands of years ago, by different civilizations, into groups of stars that take the form of animals or mythical figures. These constellations are still in use today.

⑪

⑩

⑬

⑫

⑮

⑭

The pictures below show Polaris from different locations on Earth, and at different times of the year. Find Polaris from each location. Draw a line from the boy to show which direction is north.

If there were a line going through the Earth's axis and coming out of the North Pole, it would point directly at the star Polaris, also called the **North Star**. Because of this, Polaris is the only star in the sky that's always in the same place from anywhere we look, so it can be used for navigation purposes. Polaris can be found with the help of the Big Dipper. Follow an imaginary line that continues from the two stars on the end of the "dipper" until you reach the next star. That is **Polaris**, the North Star.

⑯

⑰

⑱

During which seasons do we see the other three positions if they appear to be moving counter-clockwise around Polaris?

This is how the constellations surround Polaris.

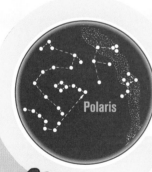

spring

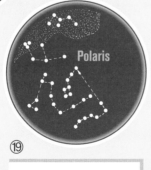
⑲

⑳

⑳ Polaris
㉑

Grade 6 ANSWERS

Math

1 Whole Numbers

1a. 1171
 b. One thousand one hundred seventy-one
 c. 1171 ; 1000 ; 100 ; 70 ; 1
2a. 74 899
 b. Seventy-four thousand eight hundred ninety-nine
 c. 74 899 = 70 000 + 4000 + 800 + 90 + 9
3a.
```
      3 2 8
  x     7 6
  -------
    1 9 6 8
  2 2 9 6 0
  -------
  2 4 9 2 8
```
 b. Twenty-four thousand nine hundred twenty-eight
 c. 24 928 = 20 000 + 4000 + 900 + 20 + 8
4a.
```
        2 0 5
  14 ) 2 8 7 0
       2 8
       ----
          7 0
          7 0
```
 b. Two hundred five   c. 205 = 200 + 5
 5. 19 072 ; 18 000
 6. 12 096 ; 200 ; 60 ; 12 000
 7. 19 350 ; 200 ; 90 ; 18 000
 8. 34 967 ; 500 ; 70 ; 35 000
 9. 135R2 ; 6500 ; 50 ; 130   10. 274 ; 5200 ; 20 ; 260
11. 77R14 ; 4800 ; 60 ; 80   12. 92R9 ; 3000 ; 30 ; 100
13. 14 277   14. 54 539   15. 11 871   16. 8438
17. 17 820   18. 207R26   19. 7722   20. 236R14
21. 27 002   22. 107R33
23. 3268 ÷ 64 = 51R4 ; There are 51 chocolate eggs in each basket. 4 are left.
24. 125 x 52 = 6500 ; Amy buys 6500 chocolate eggs in all.
25. 18 682 + 4753 = 23 435 ; The store orders 23 435 bags in all.
26. 268 x 12 = 3216 ; Uncle Tom will get $3216.
27. 10 382 – 7826 = 2556 ; That bag of chocolate eggs is 2556 g.
28. 32 ; 12 ; 20   29. 25 ; 10 ; 35   30. 50 ; 13 ; 37
31. 32 + 15 ; 47   32. 11 – 3 ; 8   33. 36 + 7 ; 43
34. 56 – 7 ; 49   35. 30 + 20 ; 50   36. 8 + 21 ; 29
37. 50 – 3 x 9 = 23 ; His change is $23.
38. 84 ÷ 3 – 9 =19 ; He has 19 marbles left.
39. 20 + 17 x 2 = 54 ; She has $54.

2 Decimals

 1. 10 + 6 + 0.2 + 0.05 + 0.008 ; 16 and 258 thousandths
 2. 20 + 3 + 0.1 + 0.07 + 0.004 ; 23 and 174 thousandths
 3. 40 + 0.01 + 0.009 ; 40 and 19 thousandths
 4. 4.958, 8.549, 9.548, 9.854
 5. 4.102, 4.201, 10.204, 10.402
 6. 3.157, 3.175, 3.715, 3.751
 7.
```
  0.003  0.008      0.019 0.024    0.031  0.036
  |--|--|--|--|--|--|--|--|--|--|--|--|--|--|
  0        0.01      0.02      0.03      0.04
```
 8. 10.593   9. 3.214   10. 6.522   11. 1.752
12. 1.731   13. 5.973   14. 3.424   15. 5.995
16. 8.575   17. 2.016   18. 4.665   19. 3.566
20. 8.329 + 4.378 = 12.707
21. 460   22. 32.93   23. 1.8   24. 147

25. 31.53   26. 206   27. 83.88   28. 13.68
29. 52.98   30. 7.626   31. 7.735   32. 24.944
33. 1.084   34. 0.562   35. 2.309   36. 46.25
37. 60.15   38. 3.014   39. 4.33   40. 0.2
41. 1.65   42. 0.256   43. 0.025   44. 0.54
45. 0.37   46. 0.4
47.
```
        1 8.3
   6 ) 1 0 9.8
       6
       ---
       4 9
       4 8
       ---
         1 8
         1 8
```
48.
```
         2 2.7 4
   8 ) 1 8 1.9 2
       1 6
       ---
         2 1
         1 6
         ---
           5 9
           5 6
           ---
             3 2
             3 2
```
49.
```
        1 6.8 3
   5 ) 8 4.1 5
       5
       ---
       3 4
       3 0
       ---
         4 1
         4 0
         ---
           1 5
           1 5
```
50. 7.33   51. 35.08   52. 4.87   53. 28.88
54. 2.53   55. 41.57   56. 75.06   57. 10.68
58. 107.55   59. 20.04
60. 4 x 0.325 = 1.3 ; They weigh 1.3 kg in all.
61. 11.16 ÷ 9 = 1.24 ; It is $1.24.
62. 0.56 ÷ 7 = 0.08 ; It is 0.08 kg.
63. 4.95 + 6.49 = 11.44 ; He needs to pay $11.44.
64. 3 x 11.16 = 33.48 ; He needs to pay $33.48.
65. 20 – 4.95 = 15.05 ; His change is $15.05.
66. 1.90

3 Fractions, Percent, and Ratio

 1. $1\frac{2}{3}$ 2. $3\frac{1}{5}$ 3. $\frac{9}{2}$ 4. $\frac{23}{7}$
 5. $\frac{9}{5}$ 6. $1\frac{1}{7}$ 7. $\frac{11}{4}$ 8. $\frac{31}{10}$
 9. $1\frac{7}{8}$ 10. $1\frac{5}{6}$
11. >   12. <   13. >   14. >
15. >   16. <
17. $\frac{3}{4}$, $1\frac{1}{2}$, $\frac{5}{2}$ 18. $1\frac{6}{7}$, $2\frac{1}{7}$, $\frac{19}{7}$
19. $1\frac{3}{5}$, $\frac{19}{10}$, $3\frac{1}{10}$ 20. $1\frac{5}{6}$, $\frac{13}{6}$, $\frac{7}{3}$
21. $\frac{3}{8}$; $\frac{4}{8}$; $\frac{7}{8}$ 22. $\frac{8}{9}$; $\frac{3}{9}$; $\frac{5}{9}$
23. $\frac{4}{12}$; $\frac{6}{12}$; $\frac{5}{6}$ 24. $\frac{3}{4}$; $\frac{1}{4}$; $\frac{1}{2}$
25. $\frac{5}{15}$; $\frac{1}{3}$ 26. $\frac{6}{10}$; $\frac{3}{5}$ 27. $\frac{16}{20}$; $\frac{4}{5}$
28. $\frac{3}{9}$; $\frac{1}{3}$ 29. $\frac{4}{8}$; $\frac{1}{2}$ 30. $\frac{4}{12}$; $\frac{1}{3}$
31. $\frac{12}{14}$; $\frac{6}{7}$ 32. $\frac{6}{8}$; $\frac{3}{4}$ 33. $\frac{12}{16}$; $\frac{3}{4}$
34. $\frac{12}{18}$; $\frac{2}{3}$ 35. $\frac{18}{24}$; $\frac{3}{4}$ 36. $\frac{13}{13}$; 1
37. $\frac{6}{10}$; $\frac{3}{5}$ 38. $\frac{14}{20}$; $\frac{7}{10}$
39. 31%   40. 86%   41. 36%
42. 25%   43. 49%   44. 6%
45. 13%   46. 85%   47. 9%
48. $\frac{60}{100}$; 60   49. $\frac{45}{100}$; 45   50. $\frac{25}{100}$; 25
51. $\frac{70}{100}$; 70   52. $\frac{17}{25}$ 53. $\frac{7}{10}$
54. $\frac{1}{2}$ 55. $\frac{9}{20}$ 56. $\frac{6}{25}$
57. $\frac{3}{10}$

58. 0.26   59. 0.4   60. 0.18   61. 0.09
62. 0.63   63. 0.55   64. 7.40   65. 3.3
66. 8.8   67. 3.67
68a. 3:5   b. 3:8   c. 5:8
69a. 5:7   b. 5:12   c. 7:12
70-75. (Suggested answers)
70. 4:14   71. 8:10   72. 16:18   73. 8:30
74. 6:20   75. 12:14   76. 1:3   77. 1:10
78. 2:3   79. 2:3   80. 3:7   81. 3:4
82. 3:4   83. 2:9   84. 3:5

4 Integers and Number Theory

1. C ; D ; A ; B ; E
2. 9   3. 1   4. -2
5. 4   6. 5   7. -2
8. -1   9. 0
10. -2°C ; 0°C ; -3°C ; -5°C ; 2°C ; -1°C ; -1°C
11. Thursday   12. Wednesday   13. 5 days
14. Tuesday   15. Friday

16-19.
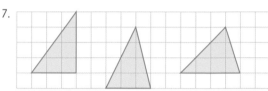

20. 3 ; 6, 12, 18, 24, 30, 36, 42, and 48
21. 3, 8 ; 24 and 48
22a. 6   b. 10   c. 40   d. 24
23. 18, 21, 24, 27,⟨30⟩; 25,⟨30⟩ 35, 40, 45, 50 ; 15
24. 4, 8,⟨12⟩ 16, 20,⟨24⟩ 28, 32,⟨36⟩ 40 ;
    6,⟨12⟩ 18,⟨24⟩ 30,⟨36⟩ 42, 48, 54, 60 ; 12
25. 12 ; 6 ; 4   26. 20 ; 10 ; 5
27. 16 ; 8 ; 4   28. 36 ; 18 ; 12 ; 9 ; 2
29. 24 ; 12 ; 8 ; 6   30. 48 ; 24 ; 16 ; 12 ; 8
31a. 1, 2, 3, 4, 6, 12   b. 1, 2, 4, 5, 10, 20
  c. 1, 2, 4, 8, 16   d. 1, 2, 3, 4, 6, 9, 12, 18, 36
  e. 1, 2, 3, 4, 6, 8, 12, 24
  f. 1, 2, 3, 4, 6, 8, 12, 16, 24, 48
32. 1, 2, 4 ; 4   33. 1, 2, 4 ; 4
34. 1, 2, 3, 4, 6, 8, 12, 24 ; 24   35. 17, 29, 41, 73, 97
36.

3 ; 3

37.
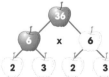
2 x 2 x 3 x 3

38.
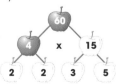
2 x 2 x 3 x 5

39.
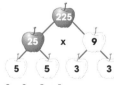
3 x 3 x 5 x 5

5 Measurement

1. (13 + 15) x 2 ; 56 ; 15 x 12 ; 180
2. 15 + 10 + 18 ; 43 ; (18 x 9) ÷ 2 ; 81
3. (12 + 10) x 2 ; 44 ; 10 x 10 ; 100
4. 10 + 15 + 8 ; 33 ; (8 x 9) ÷ 2 ; 36
5. 10 + 9 + 4 ; 23 ; (9 x 4) ÷ 2 ; 18
6-7. (Suggested answers)
6.
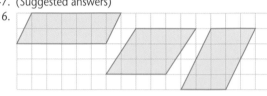
7.
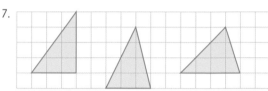

8. 32   9. 36   10. 8   11. 57
12. A: 320   B: 540   C: 16   D: 768
    E: 40   F: 70   G: 324
13. 4   14. 15   15. 6   16. 12.5
17. 324   18. 216   19. kg   20. mg
21. g   22. mg   23. g   24. kg
25. 2000   26. 0.25   27. 6800   28. 4
29. 3000   30. 0.4   31. 500   32. 6
33. 95   34. 4   35. 50

6 Geometry

1.

2.

3.

4.

5.

6.

7.

8.

9.

10.

11.

12.

13. 4   14. 3   15. 2
16. 5   17. 4   18. 6
19. (Suggested answer)   20.

21.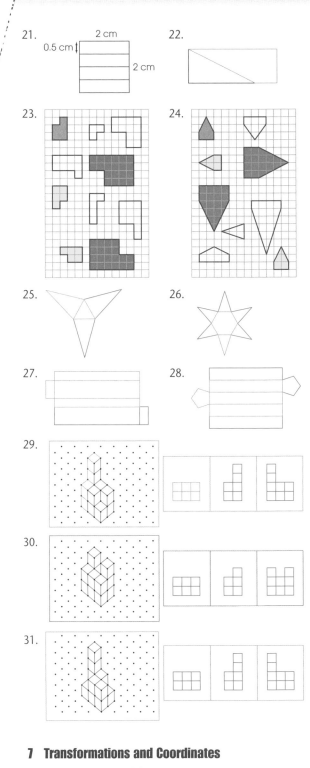

22.

23.

24.

25.

26.

27.

28.

29.

30.

31.

7-9.

10a-b. 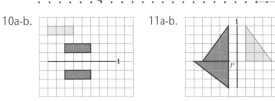   11a-b.

c. Translation   c. Yes

12a-b. 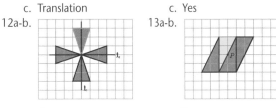   13a-b.

c. 4   c. Yes

14-18.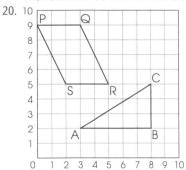

14. (2,3), (3,2), (3,1), (1,1), and (1,2)
15. (8,3), (9,2), (9,1), (7,1), and (7,2)
16. (3,4), (4,5), (5,5), (5,3), and (4,3)
17. (13,4), (12,3), (11,3), (11,5), and (12,5)
19. (Suggested answer)
    Rotate D a quarter turn counterclockwise about (11,3).
    Then translate it 8 units left and 2 units down.

20.

21. A triangle   22. A parallelogram
23. 7.5   24. 12
25. It will be (0,5). It is a trapezoid.
26. (5,3)
27a. 500   b. 200

8 Patterns and Simple Equations

1. 67 ; 131 ; 259 ; D   2. 143 ; 287 ; 575 ; A
3. 14 ; 12 ; 11 ; C   4. 203 ; 608 ; 1823 ; B
5. 47 ; 95 ; 191 ; Double the previous number and add 1.
6. 18 ; 34 ; 66 ; Double the previous number and minus 2.
7. 26 ; 12 ; 5 ; Divide the previous number by 2 and minus 1.

7 Transformations and Coordinates

1. 3 units up, 3 units left
2. 4 units down, 5 units right   3. 5 units left
4-6.

8.
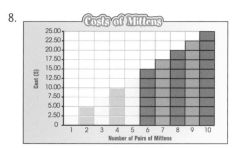

9. 8   10. 17.50   11. 30

12. If the number of pairs of mittens increases by 1, the cost will be $2.50 more.

13. Yes. The cost of mittens will increase by $2 if the number of pairs of mittens goes up by 1.

14a. The number of pairs of mittens that the next customer buys is equal to the sum of those the 2 previous customers bought.

b. 21

15a. 150 ; 175   b. Saturday   c. 225 coupons
16a. 280 ; 340   b. 7:00 p.m.   c. 460 km
17a. 320 ; 384   b. 8 bracelets   c. 640 beads
18. 4 x y = 20 ; 5   19. y − 3 = 9 ; 12
20. y + 5 = 15 ; 10   21. 50 ÷ y = 10 ; 5
22. 9.6   23. 26   24. 16.88   25. 48
26. 2   27. 5   28. 50
29. 100   30. 120   31. 12

9 Data Management

1a. $\frac{1}{6}$ b. $\frac{1}{12}$ c. $\frac{1}{2}$ d. $\frac{1}{4}$
2. 2   3. Yellow   4. Blue
5. Red: 4 ; Yellow: 2 ;
   Blue: 12 ; Purple: 6

6. **Colour of Paper Flowers**

7. 80 ; 30 ; 65 ; 45
Favourite Drinks of the People

8. Pop   9. Milk   10. No   11. 125 girls

12. (Suggested answer)
"Others" column includes drinks that are not on the list in the table, e.g. water.

13.

14. September   15. 100
16. The sale decreased.
17. The sale was stable from Jan to Apr, but it decreased in May and Jun.
18. 700 pizzas
19. 2 ; 2 ; 1   20. 16 ; 14.5 ; 12
21. 15.34 ; 15.67 ; 18.25   22. 6.1 ; 6.4 ; 6.4
23. 1, 5, 9, 9

10 Probability

1. D   2. B   3. E
4. C   5. A

6. ; $\frac{7}{8}$ 7. ; $\frac{1}{2}$

8. ; $\frac{1}{2}$ 9. ; $\frac{1}{2}$

10.
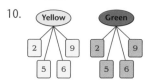

11. 12   12. Yes

13a. $\frac{1}{12}$ b. $\frac{1}{12}$ c. $\frac{1}{3}$ d. $\frac{1}{4}$
e. $\frac{1}{4}$ f. $\frac{1}{6}$ g. $\frac{1}{6}$

14. 5 times

15.
Hamburger	Salad	Cake / Ice cream
	Fries	Cake / Ice cream
	Baked potato	Cake / Ice cream
Sandwich	Salad	Cake / Ice cream
	Fries	Cake / Ice cream
	Baked potato	Cake / Ice cream

16. 12   17. 6   18. 4
19a. $\frac{1}{12}$ b. $\frac{1}{12}$ c. 0

Review

```
1.        2 6.4
     6 ) 1 5 8.4
          1 2
          3 8
          3 6
            2 4
            2 4
```

```
2.        1 4.2 2
     8 ) 1 1 3.7 6
          8
          3 3
          3 2
            1 7
            1 6
              1 6
              1 6
```

```
3.          9.7 8
     2 ) 1 9.5 6
          1 8
          1 5
          1 4
            1 6
            1 6
```

4.
```
       7.88
   9 ) 7 0.9 2
       6 3
       7 9
       7 2
         7 2
         7 2
```

5.
```
       8.1 6
   5 ) 4 0.8
       4 0
         8
         5
         3 0
         3 0
```
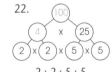

6.
```
       5.6 9
   3 ) 1 7.0 7
       1 5
         2 0
         1 8
           2 7
           2 7
```

7. $2\frac{3}{5}, 3\frac{1}{5}, \frac{19}{5}$

8. $\frac{9}{8}, 1\frac{5}{8}, \frac{16}{8}$

9. $1\frac{3}{4}, 2\frac{1}{4}, \frac{11}{4}$

10. $1\frac{2}{3}, 2\frac{1}{3}, 2\frac{2}{3}$

11. $\frac{12}{10}$; $1\frac{1}{5}$

12. $\frac{4}{20}$; $\frac{1}{5}$

13. $\frac{12}{7}$; $1\frac{5}{7}$

14. $\frac{4}{3}$; $1\frac{1}{3}$

15. $\frac{6}{15}$; $\frac{2}{5}$

16. $\frac{6}{8}$; $\frac{3}{4}$

17. $\frac{16}{12}$; $1\frac{1}{3}$

18. $\frac{9}{9}$; 1

19. $\frac{8}{16}$; $\frac{1}{2}$

20. $\frac{4}{6}$; $\frac{2}{3}$

21.
```
        (105)
     (35) x (3)
  (5) x (7) x (3)
```
3 ; 5 ; 7

22.
```
          (100)
      (4)  x  (25)
  (2) x (2) x (5) x (5)
```
2 ; 2 ; 5 ; 5

23. 973

24.
```
       4 0 9
   x     6 3
     1 2 2 7
   2 4 5 4 0
   2 5 7 6 7
```

25. 2504

26. 135 + 23 = 158
27. 44 – 7 = 37
28. 30 + 4 = 34
29. 8 + 16 = 24
30. 70 – 5 = 65
31. 16 + 16 = 32
32. 2304 cm³
33. 1620 cm³
34. 240 cm³
35. A
36. 2
37. 200
38. 46 + 3 x 16 = 94 ; He will have 94 stickers in all.
39. 3 x 4.95 = 14.85 ; 3 packs of stickers cost $14.85.
40. 4 ; 6 ; 2 ; 12 ; $\frac{1}{6}$; $\frac{1}{4}$; $\frac{1}{12}$; $\frac{1}{2}$

41.

Coloured Pencils

42. 2
43. 3
44a. $\frac{1}{6}$ b. $\frac{1}{12}$ c. $\frac{1}{4}$ d. $\frac{1}{2}$
45. A red pencil
46. 0
47. A: (0,3) B: (1,9) C: (3,5)
    D: (6,0) E: (7,9) F: (7,5)
    G: (10,4) H: (10,0) I: (11,11)
48. E and F
49. Trapezoid
50. C ; 2 units left
51. Triangle
52. (6,0), (2,0), and (2,4)
53. (6,8), (6,4), and (10,4)
54a. 2500 ; 4900 b. Aug 28 c. 38 500 visitors
55. 4.20
56. 360
57a. 2 : 3 b. 2 : 5 c. 3 : 5

58.
Fraction	$\frac{3}{10}$	$\frac{4}{25}$	$\frac{3}{5}$	$\frac{9}{50}$	$\frac{7}{20}$
Decimal	0.3	0.16	0.6	0.18	0.35
Percent	30%	16%	60%	18%	35%

English

1 Asteroids

A. 1. B 2. C 3. A 4. B
    5. C 6. C 7. C 8. C
    9. B 10. A

B. 1. extinction 2. catastrophe 3. deflecting
    4. orbit 5. region 6. formation
    7. extensive 8. research 9. observe
    10. statistics 11. likelihood 12. fraction
    13. community 14. strategy 15. avoidable

C. 1. adjectives : numerous ; visible ; small
       adverb : clearly
    2. adjective : high-speed
       adverb : frequently
    3. adjectives : tremendous ; speeding ; small
       adverb : eventually
    4. adjective : smaller
       adverb : scientifically
    5. adjectives : stony ; difficult ; ordinary
       adverb : extremely
    6. adjectives : naked ; huge
       adverb : barely

2 The World's Most Famous Doll

A. Paragraph 1 : ✔ 3   Paragraph 2 : ✔ 2
    Paragraph 3 : ✔ 1   Paragraph 4 : ✔ 1
    Paragraph 5 : ✔ 1

B. 1. New York Toy Fair ; 1959 2. 3 ; 10,000
    3. over 80 4. 1961
    5. over 40

C. 1. F 2. C 3. C 4. C
    5. F 6. C 7. C 8. C

D. 1. of the celebrity Barbies
    2. of the creators ; of Barbie ; in 1959
    3. In 1964 ; of age
    4. of Barbie ; until 1965
    5. in the Olympics ; against an Olympic swimmer
    6. of Barbie ; in more than 150 countries ; around the world
    7. of all time
    8. on "Totally Hair" Barbie ; from head ; to toe
    9. In the year 1999 ; with in-line skates
    10. to Barbie's wardrobe

3 Shopping Malls

A. 1. F 2. O 3. O 4. F
    5. O 6. F 7. F 8. F
    9. O 10. O 11. F 12. F

Your Opinion
    (Individual answer)

B. 1. <u>After watching the movie,</u> (they went for a bite to eat).
    2. <u>Because it started to rain,</u> (the race was cancelled).
    3. <u>If his team win this game,</u> (they win the championship).
    4. (She invited her friends to her house) <u>before they left for the party.</u>
    5. (It snowed heavily) <u>while they were driving home.</u>
    6. <u>Whenever they met,</u> (they had a long chat).

C. (Answers will vary.)
1. Because the circus came to town, they were absent from school.
2. They played cards when he invited his friends over.
3. When the teacher asked for everyone's attention, the students were quiet.
4. Because she forgot her books at school, she will not be able to do her homework.
5. Because the fog rolled in, it became difficult to see.
6. They were stranded on the highway when the car broke down.

D. looking → browsing ; numerous → plentiful ;
normal → common ; As a result → Consequently ;
perfect → ideal ; rarity → phenomenon ;
unbearable → insufferable ; appeared → sprouted up ;
collection → spectrum

4 Skateboarding

A. 1. It is a hands-free jump.
2. They consisted of roller-skate wheels attached to 2-by-4 planks.
3. They applaud one another's efforts and appreciate any new standard set for them to reach.
4. Makaha produced the first professional skateboard.
5. It was banned for the following reasons: fatal accidents, frequent injuries, and a dislike of the sport by the general public.
6. Urethane wheels meant higher safety and better performance.
7. They like to practise on residential streets, at office tower concourses, and anywhere where steps and railings can be found.
8. Skate parks, televised competitions, sophisticated equipment, trade publications, and specialized clothing helped make skateboarding a mainstream sport.
9. Skateboarders are competitive but they also support and applaud one another.
10. They had handles attached for balance.

B. (Answers may vary.)
1. Is it better to mind your own business or is it appropriate to speak your mind?
2. The boys played baseball in the schoolyard but the bell rang and they were called back to class.
3. Students were called to an assembly in the gymnasium and the principal spoke to them about safety.
4. She invited everyone to her birthday party but not everyone was able to show up.

Challenge
(Answers will vary.)
1. When the wind was blowing fiercely, the waves crashed against the bow and the sailboat dipped and swayed.
2. When the grade six students put on a school play, the gymnasium was filled with spectators and everyone enjoyed the performances.

C. 2. careful   3. formation   4. disabled
5. cancellation   6. competitive   7. unable
8. unexpectedly

5 The Canadian Comedy Icon

A. 1. T   2. F   3. F   4. F
5. F   6. T   7. T   8. F
9. F   10. T   11. F   12. F

B. 1. He got his inspiration from his parents.
2. Austin Powers was created by combining popular characters such as Inspector Clouseau, Matt Helm, and James Bond.
3. He often entertained his friends by creating comical characters.

C. (Individual writing)
D. (Individual writing)
E. (Individual writing)
F. (Answers may vary.)
1. transcribe ; inscription
2. transportation ; importing
3. submit ; remit
4. statue ; status
5. incredible ; credible
6. reversible ; convertible

Challenge
(Answers will vary.)
1. moveable from one place to another; easy to carry
2. sending something from one place to another
3. believability; honesty

6 The Building of Disneyland

A. 1. He wanted to build the "Magic Kingdom" so that children and their parents could experience the fantasy world of Disney.
2. The three problems that had to be solved were: what the park would consist of, where it would be built, and how to pay for it.
3. The breaking out of World War II delayed Disney's building plans.
4. At first he thought he would need only 8 acres but eventually he purchased 160 acres.
5. He promoted it through his TV show "Disneyland".
6. The five areas of "Magic Kingdom" are: Main Street, Adventureland, Frontierland, Fantasyland, and Tomorrowland.
7. It took two years and 17 million dollars to build the "Magic Kingdom".
8. The four problems on opening day were: local residents protested the opening of the park, plumbers were on strike causing a water shortage, the high temperature caused the asphalt to melt making it difficult to walk on, and nearly 30,000 counterfeit tickets were discovered.

B. 1. is   2. surprises   3. appears
4. are   5. entertains   6. is
7. are   8. were

C. 1. go   2. play   3. is
4. starts   5. walk   6. are
7. match   8. enjoy

D. 1. border ; boarder   2. red ; read
3. pores ; pours   4. feet ; feat
5. suede ; swayed   6. sale ; sail
7. hear ; here   8. paws ; pause

7 Earthquakes

A. 1. B 2. B 3. C 4. C
5. A 6. C 7. D 8. A
9. D 10. A
B. 1. C 2. INC 3. INC 4. C
5. INC 6. INC 7. C 8. C
C. 1. INC 2. INC 3. INC 4. C
5. C 6. C 7. C 8. C
D. 1. murky 2. bright 3. exotic
4. freezing 5. stench 6. succulent
7. crunchy 8. hiss

8 Stephanie Dotto – Making a Difference

A. 1. 1,500 2. 80 3. 200 4. 2000
5. 1,000 6. 37 7. 200 8. 6,000
9. 500 10. 3
B. (Individual writing)
C. 1. destiny 2. poor 3. duration
4. equal 5. ruined 6. sickened
7. devotion 8. defeat 9. businesses
10. knowledge
D. 1. corporations 2. impoverished 3. overcome
4. devastated 5. expertise 6. dedication
7. infected 8. fate
E. 1. Mr. Johnson worked with Uncle Bob at the Acme Leather Company.
2. She read the Bible on Sunday and went to St. Joseph's Church.
3. The book Cat in the Hat was written by Dr. Seuss.
4. Mike Myers starred in the film "Wayne's World".
5. Samuel de Champlain established a settlement at Quebec City in 1608.
6. Professor Smith taught English at the University of Toronto.
7. The Mona Lisa, arguably the world's most famous painting, is on display in The Louvre in Paris.
8. Her birthday, January 2nd, is the day after New Year's Day.

9 The Blackout

A. (Answers may vary.)
1. Streetcars were not running.
2. A massive blackout across the north east United States and much of Ontario
3. Hospitals cancelled surgeries.
4. Elevators were not running.
5. City lights were out.
6. People rushed to stores to stock up on canned and packaged goods.
7. People got information from battery-operated radios.
8. Traffic lights were out.
9. People were stranded in subway tunnels.
B. On Monday, September 9, a new student was admitted to our class. Our teacher, Mr. Peters, asked for the attention of the class. "Class," he said, "I would like to introduce Aisha Williams, a new student to our school." Instantly, everyone turned and looked at the timid, frightened girl by the door. Being a new student, anyone would admit, is not easy. After she was introduced, she sat in her seat near the back of the room. Suddenly, the recess bell rang, and everyone got up to get their coats. At recess, students have the following choices: play in the yard, go to the library, help teachers in the younger grades, or answer phones in the office. A few of the students went up to Aisha, introduced themselves, and invited her to play in the yard. As expected, she was shy at first but, after a few minutes, a big smile came to her face. Unfortunately, just as she was getting comfortable playing with her new friends, the bell rang again.
C. (Answers may vary.)
1. most talented 2. critical 3. determine
4. championship 5. circled 6. approach
7. stunned 8. awestruck 9. swayed
10. nervous 11. anticipation 12. silent
13. wound up 14. blistering 15. dove
16. extended 17. lightning 18. ricocheted
19. bounced 20. trickled 21. flickered
22. roared

10 World Idol

A. 1. B ; C ; A 2. B ; C ; A 3. C ; A ; B
B. 1. G 2. D 3. H 4. I
5. B 6. J 7. F 8. E
9. A 10. C
C. Once a month, usually on a Friday, the teacher held a spelling contest. Many of the words were difficult to spell: some impossible. The following examples are typically difficult words: pneumonia, tonsillitis, recommendation, and magnificence. The teacher would read out the words; the students would anxiously await their turn. A student would get two tries at a correct spelling: a wrong answer meant you had to be seated. It was exciting; however, it was also nerve-racking. When it came down to the final word, there was silence: no one moved. Even if you were no longer in the contest, it was still exciting; we would watch the final two contestants battle it out. Often a different person would win: this is what made it fun. The teacher had one purpose in this contest: students learning new words. The students had their own purpose: winning the contest.
D. (Individual answers)
Challenge
(Suggestions only)
1. died 2. screamed
3. smiled 4. whispered

Review

A. Jenny and Samantha who were best friends decided to organize a skating party at the local arena. They intended to rent the arena and (wisely) charge everyone a small admission fee. Everyone (enthusiastically) responded (immediately). (Initially) they thought that they would have great difficulty selling the necessary one hundred tickets but it was (surprisingly) easy. The first thing they did was sell tickets to their classmates and (cleverly) suggest that they (all) bring a neighbourhood friend or a favourite relative. (Next), they posted an attractive sign outside the gymnasium. (Soon) half the tickets were sold. On the final day before the event, the last ticket was (finally) sold. The party was exciting. The popular music played (loudly) over the arena speakers and everyone had a wonderful time. Jenny and Samantha (proudly) declared that this would be an annual event.

B. 1. E   2. D   3. B   4. A
    5. C
C. 1. F   2. C   3. F   4. F
    5. C   6. C   7. F   8. F
D. Paul lives (in the city) and his cousin, Roger, lives (in the country). (During the holidays), Paul invited Roger to visit him (in the city). The trip into town took (over two hours) of highway driving. Roger, a boy from a farm, was amazed (at the size) of the tall buildings in the downtown core. He was used to open fields of corn, trails for horseback riding, and skies filled (with stars) (at night). (After his visit), he suggested to Paul that (in the summer) he come (to the farm) and enjoy two weeks of a complete lifestyle change.
E. If you live in Toronto and you watch NHL hockey, chances are you are a Maple Leafs fan. You may even be lucky enough to get tickets to the Air Canada Centre to watch a game. Every Saturday night, thousands of fans make their way to Lakeshore Boulevard to see their beloved Leafs.
F. 1. poor   2. ruined   3. endurance
    4. companies   5. pictures   6. destiny
G. 1. Take   2. Can   3. raise
    4. lay   5. let
H. 1. accept   2. fewer   3. among
    4. into   5. take
I. 1. G   2. P   3. P
    4. P   5. G   6. P
J. 1. (Before the guests arrived), they set the table.
    2. They bought a new car (because they were making a long trip).
    3. (If you don't dress warmly in this weather), you will freeze.
    4. (Whenever they exercise vigorously), they work up a sweat.
    5. The students were relieved (after they had written the test).
K. 1. C   2. CC   3. C
    4. CC   5. C
L. 1. is   2. were   3. walk
    4. play   5. were
M. 1. border   2. pause   3. feat
    4. suede   5. teas
N. 1. simile   2. personification
    3. personification   4. personification
    5. alliteration   6. simile
O. 1. Before they bought their skis, they compared prices.
    2. She collected the following items: antique dolls, stamps, and clocks.
    3. The school is concerned with one thing: the success of all students.
    4. She was a volleyball player; her brother preferred to play hockey.
    5. Students should be hardworking, not lazy.
    6. The final game, they all agreed, was the best game of the season.
    7. Paul, his best friend, lived next door.

Science

1 Invertebrates

1. Invertebrates: snail, jellyfish, octopus, earthworm, centipede, grasshopper
   Vertebrates: dog, turtle, hawk, snake, human being, shark

2. CB   3. WB   4. WB   5. CB
6. CB   7. CB   8. WB   9. CB
10. WB   11. WB   12. WB
13 A. sponges   B. sea anemones
   C. worms   D. mollusks
   E. arthropods   F. sand dollars
14. A   15. B   16. C
17. E   18. D   19. F
20. arthropod   21. Insects
22. exoskeleton   23. sense organs
24. three   25. thorax
26. legs   27. dragonfly
28. cockroach
29.   30.   31.   32.

2 Diverse Vertebrates

1. Amphibian ; B, C   2. Mammal ; F, H
3. Reptile ; D, J   4. Fish ; G, I
5. Bird ; A, E
6. A. Cheetah   B. Duck   C. Elephant
   D. Snake   E. Frog   F. Fish
7. (Answers will vary.)
8. flick and stick ; D   9. bite and tear ; A
10. filter ; B   11. chew ; F
12. sip ; E   13. grab and swallow ; C
14. Brown Banded Bamboo Shark ; No
15. Wood Frog ; No
16. Sea Turtle ; No
17. African Elephant ; Yes
18. Great Blue Heron ; Yes

3 Air: All about It

1. bubble filled with air, chimney smoke blown sideways, kite in air, balloon filled with air, hair dryer blowing on hair, pinwheel moving, candle flames being blown out, wind blowing hat off, basketball filled with air
2. Water heats air in the bottle, air expands, and it starts to fill the balloon.
3. Air cools and compresses and the balloon is empty again.
4. rises   5. on
6. bottom   7. warm
8. insulating   9. compressed
10. insulating   11. insulating
12. compressed   13. compressed
14. compressed   15. insulating
16. D   17. G   18. E   19. A
20. F   21. C   22. B

4 How Things Fly

1. lower ; greater
2.
3.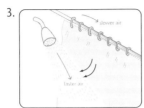
4. C   5. D   6. A
7. B   8. F   9. E
10.   11.
12. A   13. B
14. ✔   15. ✔   16.
17.   18. ✔   19. ✔
20.   21.
22.   23.
24.

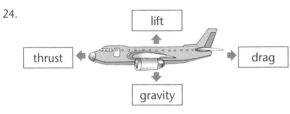

lift
thrust ◄ ► drag
gravity

25. thrust ; lift

5 Electricity

1. S   2. C   3. S   4. C
5. S   6. C   7. S   8. S
9. Conductor: water, fork, can, lemonade
   Insulator: paper, straw, twig, eraser
10. conductor   11. conductor
12. insulator   13. insulator
14. light bulb   15. wire
16. switch   17. cell
18.   19.

Correction Pen

20.   21. closed circuit

22.

23. closed circuit

24. single   25. series
26. parallel   27. power source
28. Parallel: B, D
    In series: A, C
29. The pathway would be broken and the current of electricity would be unable to flow. The other light would not operate.
30. The pathway to the other light would remain open to the flow of electricity. The other light would still operate.

6 More about Electricity

1. F   2. T   3. T   4. F
5. F   6. F   7. T
8. Solar ; renewable   9. Nuclear ; non-renewable
10. Wind ; renewable   11. Coal ; non-renewable
12. Moving water ; renewable
13. Oil ; non-renewable
14. E   15. A   16. D   17. B
18. G   19. F   20. C
21-22. (Answers will vary.)
23.

C	C	C	A	M	A	R	U	H	I	A	G	T
I	O	T	D	F	K	T	N	D	A	W	T	
R	N	L	G	J	N	S	O	L	E	M	C	
C	D	O	A	T	U	B	V	L	J	M	I	
U	U	V	E	L	B	A	W	E	N	E	R	
I	C	W	A	R	N	I	S	L	M	W	T	
T	T	T	F	I	N	Z	V	L	T	S	C	
N	O	N	R	E	N	E	W	A	B	L	E	
R	R	D	R	W	S	E	I	R	E	S	L	
O	S	R	P	S	G	K	H	A	L	X	E	
V	U	O	S	T	R	X	T	P	F	Y	A	
C	B	A	T	T	E	R	Y	L	C	E	Q	

7 Motion

1. Linear   2. Rotational
3. oscillating   4. Reciprocating
5. linear   6. oscillating
7. reciprocating   8. rotational
9.

A   B   C

D   E   F

Grade 6 ANSWERS

10. Linear: C   Oscillating: B
     Rotational: D, F   Reciprocating: A, E
11. reduce ; A   12. increase ; B
13. reduce ; A   14. increase ; B
15. A. FRICTION   B. RECIPROCATING
     C. FORCE   D. MOTION
     1. ROTATIONAL   2. OSCILLATING
     3. LINEAR

8   Motion and Machines

1. C   2. D   3. F
4. B   5. A   6. E
7. J   8. B   9. C, H
10. I, G   11. D, F   12. A, E
13. Machines using rotational motion: screw, pulley, wheel and axle
14.

15. (Answer will vary, but the fulcrum will be placed closer to the pumpkin than to the boy applying the force, and the effect force arrow should be smaller than the load force arrow.)
16. First class
17.

18. Third class
19.

20.

21.

22. (Answer will vary.)

9   Earth and Our Solar System

1. axis   2. orbit   3. northern
4. southern   5. year   6. day
7. The moon
8. New moon   9. New crescent
10. First quarter   11. Waxing gibbous
12. Full moon   13. Waning gibbous
14. Last quarter   15. Old crescent
16. (Answer will vary.)
17. moon   18. Saturn   19. Pluto
20. asteroid   21. Jupiter   22. Mars
23. Venus   24. comet   25. Earth
26. Uranus   27. Mercury   28. Neptune
29.

L	M	T	A	O	R	G	U	E	C	O	S	V
A	E	U	R	O	P	A	I	C	A	R	M	E
E	T	R	A	L	E	N	B	S	O	T	B	N
T	I	A	L	P	L	Y	S	I	T	H	E	A
S	S	I	E	N	U	M	F	N	S	E	Q	A
A	M	A	L	T	H	E	A	O	I	B	S	N
R	Q	S	K	O	N	D	E	P	L	E	D	A
D	T	E	N	N	O	E	I	E	L	V	R	N
A	T	B	H	I	M	A	L	I	A	M	F	K
R	P	A	S	I	P	H	A	E	C	V	O	E

10   The Night Sky

1. Milky Way ; D   2. Constellation ; E
3. Stars ; B   4. Planet ; A
5. Moon ; C   6. Satellite ; G
7. Northern lights ; H   8. Comet ; F
9. Meteoroids ; I
10. Draco   11. Cygnus   12. Leo
13. Cassiopeia   14. Orion   15. Pegasus
16.

17.

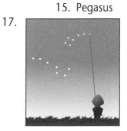

18.

19. summer   20. winter   21. fall